Versailles

Versailles

KATHRYN DAVIS

Houghton Mifflin Company

BOSTON   NEW YORK

2002

For information about permission to reproduce selections from
this book, write Permissions, Houghton Mifflin Company,
215 Park Avenue South, New York, New York 10003.

Visit our Web site: www.houghtonmifflinbooks.com.

Library of Congress Cataloging-in-Publication Data is available.
ISBN 0-618-22136-0

Book design by Anne Chalmers
Typefaces: Filosofia; Fournier

Printed in the United States of America
RRD 10 9 8 7 6 5 4 3 2 1

Grateful acknowledgment is made to *Conjunctions* and *The
Threepenny Review*, where parts of *Versailles* first appeared.

The author would also like to thank the John Simon Guggenheim Memorial
Foundation for its generous support, and Louise Glück, Regina Janes,
and Elaine Segal for their irreplaceable help with this book.

For Daphne

Architecture is merely the embellishment with which we hide our deepest needs.

—Jean Le Rond d'Alembert

Versailles

$\mathscr{M}$y soul is going on a trip. I want to talk about her. I want to talk about her. Why would anyone ever want to talk about anything else?

My soul is a girl: she is just like me. She is fourteen years old and has been promised in marriage to the French Dauphin, who also has a soul though more visible and worldly, its body already formed (so I've been told) from layers of flesh and fat. In France they piss into chamber pots made of lapis and dine on common garden slugs. In France their hands smell like vanilla and they shoot their *flèches d'amour* indiscriminately in all directions, owing to their taste for books pernicious to religion and morals.

My soul is also powerful, but like a young girl it has wishes and ideas—yes!—a soul can have ideas like a mind does. "Antonia, Antonia, you must pay attention," I can still hear Abbé Vermond implore me, waving a book in my face when all I wanted to do was dance dance dance, as if he actually believed that to be light of heart is the same as being light of head.

We traveled in a carriage coated with glass and lined with pale blue satin, beautifully swift, magnificently sprung. The end of April and the clouds compact and quick-moving, the fields turning from pale to deeper green, and the fruit trees' veiled heads humming with bees. From Vienna to Molck, from the valley of the Danube to the Castle of Nymphenburg, whose inhabitants behaved like swine. Bells pealed all along our route and uniformed men shot off guns; little girls tossed flower petals in our path. The white horses of the Danube were here one minute, gone the next; one minute we slipped into the Black Forest's long cool shadows, the next out onto a hot sunny plain.

"The world where you must pass your life is but transitory," or so advised my papa from beyond the grave. "There is naught save eternity that is without end." In my lap I had my dear little pug, the smell of whose ears will always be sweeter to me than all the perfumes of Araby and the scent of heliotrope combined.

Twenty thousand horses stabled along the road from Vienna to Strasbourg—no sooner did one of our steeds begin to lather up and stumble than it was ground into cat meat and a new one found to take its place. Serving women, hairdressers, dressmakers, surgeons, furriers, chaplains, apothecaries, cooks. Each night we managed to consume 150 chickens, 270 pounds of beef, 220 pounds of veal, 55 pounds of bacon, 50 pigeons, 300 eggs.

I was eager to please, though that meant something other than acquiesce to another's desire. Pleasing meant my own desire: the place where my body and soul met, like the musician's bow bearing down on the string, teasing a sound out: *ah ah ah ah ah!*

My soul thought she'd be happy, and then, one day, she'd die.

But, *die.*

What does this mean?

One day Antoinette will not exist, though her soul will continue to flourish.

And WHO IS THAT? WHAT IS THAT?

By the time we stopped for supper at the Abbey of Schuttern I had no appetite at all, even though the nuns tried tempting me with pilchards and apricots and kugelhopf; I admit I wept a little. It was the sixth of May; we'd been on the road for over two weeks. From my bedroom window I could see the Rhine, which looked wide and flat and the color of lead, and the light on it looked like the pilchards had, silver and skinny and unappetizing. I heard a door creak, the sound of footsteps. Angry voices arguing below, fighting over the wording in the marriage contract, by which I was to be deeded away like a cottage or a plot of land to the people of France. A fork of lightning over the Rhine, and the Lorelei's long ghostly arm lifting to meet it . . .

But Mama would never let me get away with such silly thoughts—I missed her so much I thought I'd die. "You must eat everything on your plate, Antonia. No picking and choosing. Why have you not eaten all your fish? How many times must I tell you that the child who gives in to foolish fears will never amount to much as an adult. Come here, let me take a good look at you—" peering at me through a magnifying glass. "You seem so small for your age. How is your health?" Her white white hair and her white white teeth, one of which she'd had pulled while giving birth to me. Antoinette and a decayed molar, both of us rejected by my mother's body about eight o'clock in the evening, All Souls' Day, 1755.

It was getting dark; the moon was coming up over the river. At home Carlotta would be saying her prayers and Maxie sneaking cheese to his pet mouse, poor Anna lying there with her hands folded across her chest like an effigy of herself, unable to stop coughing. Joseph and Christina, Elizabeth and Karl. Amalia, Leopold, Johanna, Josepha. Mama sitting in her private apartments, sipping her warm milk and signing state papers. Her head shorn and the walls draped in black ever since Papa's death, which she recorded in her prayer book, "Emperor Francis I, my husband, died on the 18th of August at half past nine o'clock. Our happy marriage lasted 29 years, six months and six days, 1,540 weeks, 10,781 days, 258,774 hours"—despite his numerous and humiliating infidelities.

At least I had my little pug with me, *Gott sei dank!* Tomorrow I would stop speaking German forever, but not tonight. I could see where we were headed and it was black as pitch.

GOOSEFOOT

The approach to Versailles from the east is through forests of royal hunting preserves—the Bois de Boulogne, Saint-Cloud, home to wild pigs and guinea fowl as well as the lesser forms of human life—alternating with stretches of open farmland. Here the wheat is grown that will be harvested in late summer and ground into the loaves of bread that will be viewed with "mystical respect" by the King of France himself.

The baker who bakes bread must do it properly, according to the legal standard, which states that it shall be made of the best wheat on the market or within two *deniers* of that price. And if it is found to be poorly baked or too small in size, the baker shall pay a fine of five *sols* and the bread shall be given to the poor . . .

The sky is gray. It is raining. The approach to Versailles from the east is through dense shadowy forests, the branches of the trees heavy and wet and dripping, and behind every tree a wild animal, a cutpurse, a whore. No wolves, though—the wolves are all dead and gone, hunted out of existence by Louis XIII, quite the hungry old wolf himself.

Over the Seine and onto the Avenue de Paris, the centermost of the three tree-lined roads comprising the famous *patte-d'oie,* or goosefoot, that converges at the palace gate. Rain is beading on the gold blade at the tip of each of the gate's gold rails, beading up and then streaming down to pool darkly, muddily, on the ground. No matter how frugal the reigning monarch, there never seems to be enough money. The fountains appear broken, their basins clogged with debris, and in the gardens several statues have fallen off their pedestals and are lying on their sides in the wet grass like drunkards.

A dark morning and overcast, but on the approach to the chateau no one has lit a single lantern.

The goosefoot was the idea of Le Nôtre, the Sun King's beloved gardener; he wanted to impress on the landscape the same cross the architect traces in the soil to indicate the main axes of a building. Versailles is actually a little out of alignment. The brass meridian marker traverses the Chamber of the Pendulum Clock diagonally rather than north to south, a fact no one likes to talk about because solar symbolism is crucial to the King's sense of cosmic destiny. How happy it makes him to watch the sun rise above his forecourt and set beneath his gardens! They extend on either side of the Grand Canal, endlessly unrolling toward the western horizon, where they at last slip through a gap between two poplars and plunge off the edge.

An unfortunate site for the seat of Bourbon power, really: a hillock of unstable sand in the middle of a swamp in a wind tunnel of a valley.

Of course subsequent French theoreticians have embraced the idea of Versailles's misalignment, perhaps in the same spirit with which they consider frog legs a culinary triumph.

It's always better to make something out of nothing —that's the French way.

And then the bed curtains part. How many nights? A thousand and one, give or take a few?

Though instead of telling tales I scratch my husband's flea bites, the only itch he'll let me scratch, poor thing. The bed curtains part and in he comes, my very own King of France, just as he did that first night so many years ago, his little eyes blinking uncontrollably in what I took to be a colossal effort to see me in all my tender dishabille, though I now know he was merely trying to stay awake. The sound of wind, of rain pattering onto the leaves of the orange trees, and, even at so late an hour, feet racing up and down the Stairways of the Hundred Steps.

Versailles in the spring—beloved Versailles!—frogs croaking deep within the basins of her fountains, in the puddles left by the afternoon's storm. The anguished cry of a star-crossed lover, a few far-off rumbles of thunder like dice flung across a gaming table. All the remembered sounds of my earliest acquaintance with the place, but muffled, muffled, and then, for the briefest fraction of an instant, vivid again . . .

It was my wedding night. I had just stepped out of my bridal gown embroidered with white diamonds the size of hazelnuts. The bed curtains parted and there was my new husband's face, strangely bridelike itself in its frame of white organdy and displaying the same slack-jawed expression I'd noticed earlier that evening on his grandfather's face, bored to death—as any sensible person would be—by the endless hands of cavagnole and endless trays of hors d'oeuvres, though without the old King's dark catlike eyes, his interest in female anatomy, my breasts in particular. The old King was looking straight at them as he warned his grandson not to overeat and made no effort to conceal his annoyance when Louis sagely observed that he always slept better on a full stomach.

Which is probably why he chose to bring a plum tart with him into the nuptial chamber, holding it tenderly on his palm like a pet. He took his place on the right side of the bed and, without saying a word, began to cut the tart into many tiny pieces with the same pocketknife I'd seen him use on the Host. Singing off key, a song about the hunt, *lalalalala,* and then waving the blade in my face, grudgingly, as if to suggest that if I were really hungry I could scrape clean the knife — no thank you! — with my teeth.

A tall fellow, Louis, a regular hop-pole, narrowly built and long-boned, though you could hardly tell since the lanky youth he might've been if he hadn't been forced to be King when all he really wanted was to draw maps and forge locks had already gotten swaddled in layers and layers of flesh.

If he seemed sullen on our wedding night it wasn't so much because he didn't want to share the tart with me. It wasn't even the bed he didn't want to share. It was the life.

Sweet smell of orange blossoms mixed with other less intoxicating smells, smoke in the wall hangings, shit in the hallways. Shit, not excrement, for that is how I am, have always been and always will be — I adore the vernacular!

Lean close to a man and you can smell it on him, no matter how diligently he strives to hide it. Lean close and you can also see a constellation of flea bites on the delicate skin behind the ear, but try to kiss him there — just go ahead and try — and he'll brush your lips away like *you're* the flea.

Ma petite puce, I teased, practicing my French, and through clenched teeth he replied, *Laissez-moi,* which I knew enough to know meant *Leave me alone.* Not even a flicker of humor, or that widening of the wings of the nostrils that, in my brother Karl at least, always meant he was suppressing a laugh. I crooked a finger and began to scratch first one bite, then another, until I had him moaning with pleasure. *Louder,* I prompted, because of course I knew they were all there, the Queen's Guard and a thousand revelers, laughing and drinking and fornicating on the other side of the Bull's Eye window, waiting for some sign that the Dauphin wasn't, to use his grandfather's phrase, a "laggard in the service of Aphrodite."

In those days I was also compared to Hebe, Psyche, Antiope, Flora, and Minerva, though in the case of the last less due to her braininess than the way she started life as one colossal headache.

Eventually I drew blood. *Voilà!* I said. Just a measly drop or two—but once the court laundresses spread the word, let the court gossips draw their own conclusions.

ENVELOPE

Twenty-eight by thirty-four *toises*. Thirty-two by forty. Invite carriages into the courtyard. No! Keep the horses out . . .

It was an endearing quality of the Sun King that he couldn't make up his mind.

From the beginning, of course, he knew he wanted Versailles to be the hub of the universe, and that the original chateau, a modest brick "hunting lodge" built to provide his father with the ideal setting (i.e. as far from his wife as possible) for post-hunt parties and amorous adventures, was really much too small.

On this point Louis XIV and his advisors were in perfect accord: the hub of the universe had to be a whole lot bigger. Where they hit a snag, however, was in determining the limits of filial devotion: just because he was Sun King, the advisors pointed out, didn't mean his sentimentality should be given free rein, particularly if it meant trying to find some way to cram his father's chateau into the heart of the new building like a "precious jewel," rather than tear it down like the architectural catastrophe everyone agreed it was. Tear it down? Louis roared. Am-poss-EEE-bluh! But to have to build around the old chateau would be like building around a sinkhole in a bog, the advisors whined.

It was May 1668. The Peace of Aix-la-Chapelle had just been signed and, as usual after signing a treaty, the Sun King was filled with a deep need either to start another war or begin building a monument to his own brilliance. At such moments he couldn't be stopped. Go ahead and try tearing my father's house down, he replied. As fast as you do, I'll be rebuilding it, brick by brick and stone by stone. At which point the advisors gave up. Okay, they said. Keep the stupid house. Or words to that effect.

But when you insist on cleaving to the past, no matter how enchanted your memory of it might be (through the window a round white moon and a white spray of stars and swaying among the silver branches of the lindens hundreds of yellow lanterns, and a beautiful woman with round white breasts swinging to and fro on a golden swing, playing a lute and singing, *il y a longtemps que je t'aime*, over and over, *t'aime t'aime*, as the horses whinny and stamp their hooves on the marble paving stones and the nightingales go *chook chook chook* . . .) you have to endlessly revise the present to accommodate it.

Construction began in October; the following June the King wrote a memorandum. "His Majesty wishes to make use of everything newly made," he said, by which he evidently meant that having at last seen what the beautiful and the ugly looked like sewn together (to paraphrase Saint-Simon), he'd changed his mind and wanted the old chateau razed to the ground.

But Kings are almost never left to their own devices, and Louis was lucky enough to have Jean-Baptiste Colbert as his Overseer of Buildings. Colbert, like many cold-blooded people (his emblem was a grass snake), understood the value of collaboration. Immediately he called in his fiddlers three—Le Vau, Le Brun, and d'Orbay—and together they came up with the idea of the Envelope, a revolutionary design that sprawled in the Italian manner rather than towering in the French (so as not to dwarf the old chateau but rather to embrace it, albeit diffidently), the excessive length of its walls disguised by the insertion at regular intervals of columns and pilasters, the flatness of its roof by the addition of an ornate balustrade likewise interrupted at intervals by giant sculptures of Kings riding into battle, or by cloaks and flags and sunbursts, or by gods having their way with mortal women. Like a burned-out husk of a palace, observed Saint-Simon. Or maybe more like one whose roof and final story were always just about to be built and never finished. A monument to vastness and constriction.

One hundred *toises* from the Place d'Armes to the first of two ornate golden fences, fifty *toises* from the first fence to the second, forty-two *toises* across the Royal Court and up six long steps to the Marble Court, then thirty-four to the front entrance of the Old Chateau, looking less like a precious stone set in the heart of the new building than like the monstrously big head of a monstrously long-armed baby reaching out to draw you in. According to Jean-Baptiste Colbert, this was as it should be: the King's power had to be monstrous and his palace a grasping triumph of advertising, every gorgeous thing in it, every stick of inlaid furniture, every silk swag or linen napkin, every blown-glass goblet or emerald pendant, of French manufacture.

A *toise* equals six feet; that is, two manly strides or at least eighteen of the tiny gliding footsteps required to perfectly execute the "Versailles Walk," in which the soles of a woman's slippers—a queen's diamond-soled slippers, for example, invisible beneath the hem of her Rose Bertin gown—were made to glide soundlessly across the marble so she'd look like she was floating, like she wasn't entirely human but part queen, part ghost, in preparation for things to come.

I was a pretty girl; I glittered like the morning star. My red lips would open and it was anyone's guess what would come out. A burst of song. Something by Gluck, a pretty girl in pain maybe, impaled on the horn of the moon. The Kings of France, starting with Charlemagne. A joke.

You can make yourself remember almost anything, as long as it isn't too boring.

Louis XIII. Louis XIV. Louis XV.

The Old Rogue. The Sun King. Beloved.

Louis Louis Louis Louis. Louis as far as the eye could see. And what would *my* Louis be called?

Often when my tutor was talking to me I'd picture my brain like a storm drain in a Paris street, but whenever we put on plays I always took the biggest part and never needed prompting. *War broke out after Prussian troops marched into Saxony in August of 1756. War broke out,* not, *How sweet the breeze, how bright the stars, here in the pine grove.*

At a moment's notice I could dress like a lady's maid or a courtesan or a Greek goddess. Put on an accent, sway my hips. At a moment's notice I could assume a new identity, as opposed to being forced to be a witness to history. I didn't really want to be a witness to anything, except maybe my own life as I watched it play like dappled sun across the faces of friends and loved ones.

Whereas seeing your life reflected in the face of an enemy—Madame Du Barry's face, to be specific—is more like enduring an interminable account of, say, the Punic Wars. You are denied a role, your lips criticized for being too thick, your eyes for being without eyelashes. You die before the curtain comes up.

The Du Barry had a lavishly decorated suite of rooms at the palace, linked by a secret staircase to the King's, and for the most part she remained there, nestled in his lap like a large pink baby, dispensing advice on matters of the gravest political consequence. That she hadn't a clue, that before she was Louis XV's mistress she'd been a streetwalker, and not an especially good-looking one at that, was completely beside the point.

The King adored her. "Royal," she called him. "My thweet." The lisp was said to be an affectation. On fine afternoons she'd sashay forth to take the air, her Bengali page, Zamor, trailing behind in his pink velvet jacket and trousers and his snow white turban. Sometimes he would protect her big round head from rain or sun with a frilled parasol. Sometimes she would stumble, either because she was drunk, or because she insisted on wearing shoes that were too small, or because her legs were worn out from parting for the King.

Everyone knew he couldn't get enough of her; needless to say that was all she needed to lord it over me and my poor indifferent Louis. Just as everyone knew she was the sworn enemy of the King's chief minister, Choiseul, who'd urged an alliance between France and Austria for years, as well as my marriage to the Dauphin.

Boring boring boring. Could it possibly be more boring, aside from the people themselves, or the way I felt myself slipping between events like a goldfish between lily roots?

"The King's character resembles soft wax on which the most dissimilar objects can be randomly traced," Choiseul once observed. And in fact, for all his good looks and winning ways, the King wasn't particularly smart, his three specialities being coffee making, stag hunting, and knocking the top off soft-boiled eggs.

MESDAMES

Envelope, ground floor. The apartments of Madame Adé-laïde, eldest daughter to Louis XV, King of France, also called Beloved. A beautiful morning, everything white and gold and sunstruck: couches, tables, chairs, mirrors; a chandelier, a harp.

It is the summer of 1772. Enter the King's three maiden daughters, stage right, each wearing a shapeless black gown and carrying a shapeless black workbag. The daughters are in mourning for their mother, Queen Marie Leczinska, who decided to die rather than be subjected to endless tales of her husband's infidelity.

Adélaïde and Victoire sit facing each other on matching gold brocade loveseats; Sophie scuttles across the room in her sticklike way to stand by the window.

ADÉLAÏDE: Is she coming?

SOPHIE: She is! She is!

ADÉLAÏDE: For heaven's sake, calm down. And try to remember what I told you.

VICTOIRE: Shh! Here she comes.

Enter Antoinette, stage left, in a blue silk gown that shows off her figure to excellent advantage. She too carries a workbag, of matching blue silk, and is followed by a little dog, Eggplant, the black-nosed pug she brought with her from Vienna, who immediately lifts his leg on the harp.

ANTOINETTE: Oh no. Not again.

ADÉLAÏDE: Please. Don't give it another thought.

Victoire pats the cushion beside her invitingly, but Antoinette chooses to sit on the couch, facing the audience.

ANTOINETTE: I don't understand. He's usually so good.

The women all open their bags and remove their needlework. Only Antoinette's is visible to us, a large misshapen garment in shades of rose and cream.

VICTOIRE: So, dearie, how is married life treating you? Are you getting settled in all right?

ANTOINETTE: I suppose so. I'm afraid I keep making mistakes, though. The protocol, the corsets. Everything is so different from home. *She holds up the garment, regards it ruefully.* Do you think he'll like it? It's supposed to be a vest.

SOPHIE: Father says your husband was born in a barn.

ADÉLAÏDE: That's enough, Sophie.

ANTOINETTE: No, she's right. *She sighs, furrows her pretty white brow, continues stitching.*

For a minute or two all that can be heard is the sound of thread being snipped.

ANTOINETTE: Speaking of barns, the other day I was walking under Madame Du Barry's window, and she dumped a pot of piss on me.

VICTOIRE: No!

SOPHIE: How do you know it was her?

ANTOINETTE: I recognized the bracelet.

VICTOIRE: But why would she want to do a thing like that? You've never done anything to offend her.

SOPHIE: Antoinette will be Queen one day.

Adélaïde busies herself making a knot.

ADÉLAÏDE, *offhand:* Of course now you must cut her dead. She can't be allowed to get away with such impudence.

ANTOINETTE: But she's the King's mistress. His favorite.

ADÉLAÏDE: Trust me — I understand the protocol.

SOPHIE, *giggling:* Trust me. Trust me.

ADÉLAÏDE: For the love of God, Sophie. That's enough!

SOPHIE: Uh-oh! Here comes Father.

She races from the window and takes a seat on the couch beside Antoinette, only moments before Louis, who is rakishly dressed for the hunt in a scarlet coat and leather breeches, and carrying a gilt coffeepot, enters, stage right. Immediately all three daughters begin displaying signs of agitation, fruit-lessly fussing with their hair and tugging at their clothing.

VICTOIRE: I'm starving! Have we nothing good to eat? Breakfast was a million years ago. Surely there's something left on the tray? A rind? A pit? A crust of bread?

LOUIS: You eat too much. The lot of you eat too much, and it shows. Why can't you all be more like Antoinette? *He turns to face her, staring pointedly at her chest.* Some coffee, my dear?

Meanwhile Bread, an androgynous figure in white, part baker, part winged Victory, incomplete in many respects (right cheek and ear, right hand, right foot) yet also oddly triumphant, is gradually taking shape in the gilt-framed mirror on the wall.

BREAD: Rain falls on wheat, heavy the head, bending the stalk. Harvest and crush it, thresh it and winnow it, discard the husks. Round wheat, golden wheat, round golden beads. How many beautiful women have been heroines?

ANTOINETTE: Thome coffee, Royal? My pleasure.

He was sick and getting sicker. His teeth were gone and so was his brain. He was dying and everyone knew it but no one would admit it—that was the way of the place.

The way of the place was to ignore the wages of the flesh, but still call as much attention to it as possible. Dress it up, rouge its cheeks. The flesh was interesting, especially if it was royal. So interesting the average courtier couldn't resist speculating on the size of the King's — well, *every*thing. Too interesting, in other words.

They tucked Beloved into a camp bed in his room overlooking the Marble Court, where not so very long before he'd been accustomed to watching the world come to meet him on horseback and in carriages, sun sent flying from its stirrups and gilt wheels like arrows. But now he could no longer stand the sun. It made his eyes water. Even moonlight was too much for him. He had his windows draped in yards of dark cloth, and every visit was like a game of blindman's buff.

Six doctors, five surgeons, and three apothecaries were in attendance. Six times an hour they lined up and took turns taking Beloved's pulse, studying his tongue, poking his stomach. So solemn, in their understated attire, their modest gray periwigs, gravely vying for the best place in line—it would have been amusing if it weren't for the smell. In the dark of the King's Bedchamber I could feel my poor husband tremble beside me; once Beloved was gone there'd be nothing to stand between us and our unthinkable destiny.

"I feel as though the universe were tumbling down on top of me," he said. Trembling and breathing shallowly, the way he would when I'd remove my chemise and show him my breasts, undeniably the part of me he liked best, though chiefly to gape at. And then all at once a servant lit a torch and everyone in the room gasped. My elbow jumped, knocking some fragile thing off a table and onto the floor. "Antoinette?" said Beloved, though it came out more like *nnnn*, his speech slurred, his tongue, as it turned out, covered in pustules and decomposing like the rest of him.

In the torchlight I could see his face. Like those parts of a deer that hunters discard in the woods, peeking from under dock leaves, slick and pitch-black and buzzing with flies.

"Antoinette, is that you?" he said. Cupping his privates, or what was left of them, with what was left of his hands. *Nnnnsthayoo?* And then a long horrible gurgle the First Gentleman of the King's Bedchamber translated as: "Get her out of here before she breaks something truly valuable." Lewd to the end, Beloved.

That was the last time I saw him alive. I'd been inoculated against smallpox, but Louis had not, and after that we were denied entry. Not unlike the Du Barry, though in her case it was because following his third bleeding the King knew he was going to die and decided to become pious. He sent the Du Barry away in a carriage, no doubt hoping to lend a little credibility to the confession he intended to make, his first in four decades. Poor thing! For all the trouble the woman had caused me I admit I felt sorry for her, her big empty head lolling in its usual way like a blown rose from side to side, as if her not especially slim neck wasn't up to the task of holding it aloft. Wiping her nose on her sleeve—you could tell she loved him, and if he bought her love with jewels, so what?

Whereas the daughters—no one seemed to care what became of them, least of all their father. They were ugly, anyway.

It was spring. The tenth of May. Large clouds sweeping like epic events across a clear blue sky, and the pear trees just starting to shake loose their petals, getting ready to make fruit. Bon Chrétien d'Hiver, huge and green-gold and luscious.

Everyone on tenterhooks, waiting for the slick black case to crack open and shake loose the petals of the soul.

But I'm dramatizing, as Mama would say.

Nor did Louis and I kneel together the minute the candle in Beloved's window was extinguished and pray to God for His protection. Nor did we hold hands and wail, "We are too young to reign." That is Madame Campan dramatizing, though the style of her memoir is admirable. She's the one responsible for describing how the sound of thunder filled the halls of Versailles as all the hundreds of feet of the waiting courtiers sprang into motion, racing from the Bull's Eye Chamber and down the Hall of Mirrors to pay us homage. They were the ones doing the kneeling, not us.

Of course we *were* very young: I was not yet nineteen, my husband not yet twenty. And of course we weren't especially well suited to the task ahead.

But we didn't weep—oh no. Always stolid, my Louis, always lacking in imagination. While I was all imagination, which is to say restless to the core.

The candle was extinguished, there was the sound of thunder. The black case split open and the corruption poured out; everyone leapt into his carriage and bolted for the chateau at Choisy. By four o'clock the place was empty.

Once the smallpox had run its course, fifty courtiers had caught the disease, and ten people, including the King, had died of it.

MARBLE COURT

Beginning with Louis XIII, the royal bedchamber of
every King who lived at Versailles looked out across the
Marble Court, facing east toward Paris. Even before it
was Versailles, when it was merely a glorified haymow for
Louis XIII to romp in with his girlfriends, the King's
Bedchamber was strategically positioned. Louis XV had a
secret window installed through which he could see the
world but the world couldn't see him; Louis XVI, in a rare
farsighted moment, added a telescope.

The day's first sun falls across the black and white
paving stones that give the court its name. Italian marble, luminous and fine-textured, ordered during the
second building campaign by Louis Le Vau, who'd no
sooner watched it set in place than he began to cough up
blood and die. It was his idea to lay three new steps atop
the existing two, preventing carriage access, to sink a
pool in the center of the courtyard, and to position huge

cast-iron birdcages in the corners, filled with disoriented birds from foreign lands who'd sing their exotic songs at all hours of the day and night. By the time Louis XV was lying dead in the royal bedchamber, the birdcages were gone and so was the pool, and it was once again possible to admire the perfection of Le Vau's black-and-white diaperwork pattern, especially if you shared the dead King's habit of wandering around on the roof after dark, conversing with your guests down the chimney flues.

The King is dead! Long live the King! Hours had elapsed since that cry rang through the chateau's rabbit warren of hallways, its last echoes still trapped in vast stone reservoirs far below the ground. The sun had reached the height of its arc and now was plummeting past the Lizard Fountains and into the Grand Canal, setting the windows of the Hall of Mirrors aflame and filling the Marble Court with the building's own shadow. Ordinary birds were singing, larks and warblers; most of the carriages ferrying the frightened courtiers from the house of pestilence had arrived at their destination, and everyone was letting out deep sighs of relief. Checking to make sure no unusual blemishes lurked under their face powder. Toasting their good fortune.

Meanwhile in the royal bedchamber there was work to be done.

"You must open the King's body and embalm it," said the First Gentleman of the Bedchamber to the Chief Surgeon, who knew that to do so was to sign his own death warrant.

"I will if you'll help by holding his head," the Chief Surgeon craftily replied.

And so it happened that Louis XV's heart—unlike the heart of every other King of France before him— wasn't removed from his chest cavity and pickled in herbs and spices before being sent to one of the Paris churches, where it would be accorded the kind of adoration generally reserved for a piece of the true cross. No, Beloved was buried at Saint-Denis with all his organs intact, albeit liquescent, inside him.

Nor would his heart be among those royal hearts sold during the Revolution to a painter named Martin Drolling. It was said that Drolling pounded them into "mummy," and that they lent the pigment he used in painting *L'Intérieur d'une Cuisine* (a cozy view of peasants at work) unusual brilliance and luster.

INTERIOR OF A KITCHEN

The back scullery, five A.M. A door is partly open, stage rear, letting onto a still-dark alleyway from which issues the muffled sound of furtive activity, cats or rats or God knows what.

It is the summer of 1774. Two scullery maids, both wearing juice-stained white aprons over dirty gray dresses, stand at a large work table, pitting cherries. One of them (Brigitte) is old and fat, the moonlike roundness and whiteness of her head accented by her mobcap. The other (Françoise) is young and pretty, her pale face surrounded by masses of auburn curls. The floor at the women's feet is crowded with baskets of cherries waiting to be pitted.

The door swings all the way open; enter Jean-Claude, a skinny youth with a bad complexion, carrying another basket.

JEAN-CLAUDE: This should be the last of them. *He puts the basket down, then leans against the wall so that he is facing Françoise, his arms crossed over his narrow chest.* Next it will be apricots.

BRIGITTE: Too early yet. Next will be currants.

FRANÇOISE: Same difference.

JEAN-CLAUDE: Not if you have to pick them.

Françoise pouts a little, showing off her pretty lower lip, then deepens her voice, imitating Jean-Claude.

FRANÇOISE: Not if you have to pick them. *She removes her apron and tucks the stained bib between her legs.* Who am I? Three guesses.

JEAN-CLAUDE: Give us a hint.

FRANÇOISE, *examining the bib:* Oh boohoo! Boohoo! Another month gone and once again the curse of Eve upon me!

BRIGITTE: That will do, Françoise.

JEAN-CLAUDE: I still don't get it.

FRANÇOISE, *holding the bib inches from her big blue eyes:* If I don't produce an heir soon, they'll have my head.

Jean-Claude raises his hands, palms up, and shrugs. He doesn't have a clue, and Brigitte, by the disgusted look on her full-moon face, makes it clear to the audience that the French, unlike the British, find the village idiot anything but charming.

Throughout the scene the open doorway has been gradually filling with the rosy light of dawn. A large pile of refuse becomes visible — a shapeless jumble containing here and there vaguely recognizable objects, part of a rib cage maybe, a pelvis, a forearm and hand, possibly even a head. Recumbent on the pile, the hazy figure of Bread, as far in the distance the rising sun turns Versailles butter yellow and glints off the gold blades of the palace gate.

BREAD, *singing:*

> Featherhead, featherhead
> Unfucked in your featherbed
> Twenty years and you'll be dead.

JEAN-CLAUDE: Hello? Hello? Is there anybody there?

FRANÇOISE, *dismissively:* Probably just a *croquant*, looking for a nice place to die. Monsieur (*leaving the table and calling through the door*), if you think you will find any featherbeds here you are barking up the wrong tree.

> *She exits stage rear, ostensibly to chase the offending party away, and returns with a discarded leek from the refuse pile.* I will give you one last chance. *She stares intently at Jean-Claude, positioning the drooping vegetable at her crotch and deepening her voice.* Try as I might, my insatiable sweetheart, I cannot manage to hit love's bull's-eye.

JEAN-CLAUDE, *shocked, as light finally dawns:* Oh. But that is blasphemy. They are our King and Queen. The King and Queen of France.

BREAD, *singing:*

> The King is a lout and
> The Queen is a whore

> Make them ride in the carriage
> With thirty-six doors.

Françoise ornaments her hair with the leek, as if it were a feather.

FRANÇOISE: Kiss me! Fill me with your royal broth! But wait. I forget myself. You'd rather be pounding the royal forge.

JEAN-CLAUDE: As a woman, you should be sad for her, rather than making fun.

FRANÇOISE, *pulling a solemn face:* I *am* sad for her. She is so beautiful and clever, and he is a gluttonous dullard.

BRIGITTE: Allow me to remind you that, clever or dull, they'll both have our hides if we don't get these cherries pitted. Not to mention that what they do behind the doors of the royal apartments is none of our business.

JEAN-CLAUDE: Besides, she should be glad not to be saddled like my poor little mother with as many brats as there are holes in a sieve.

BREAD, *singing:*

> Poor little mother
> Poor little brats
> Poor little Queen
> With her million hats.

$\mathbf{B}$ut oh! how exciting it was. You will have to take my word for it, really and truly exciting, the way even the smallest event of a life—like having your hair dressed, let alone being crowned Queen of France—can seem when you're young, before you've gotten a glimpse of the final shape of a thing, or even realized that final shapes exist.

When I first arrived at Versailles, everything was new to me. I would be out walking and I'd smell a flower of such astonishing sweetness it would take my breath away, and I would think, WHAT IS THAT? Or a little round object would suddenly fall on my head, and I would think, WHERE DID THAT COME FROM?

Later I'd discover that the one was jasmine from Spain, the other a black walnut from America, and I was utterly excited, as if no one had ever seen such things before.

Imagine! Antoinette, not so very different from Jacques Cartier, first Frenchman to clap eyes on a polar bear. As if a huge white creature that could devour you in one bite were the same as a walnut.

Of course I mock myself, but everyone knows what I mean. The first time you look out your window and see that it started snowing during the night and is snowing still—and when you fly down a hill on your sleigh it feels as if stars are beating against your face. You want it to happen again and again and again.

Which is how it was in the first days of my queen-hood as I watched the wardrobe women arrive with their basketloads of underclothes, handkerchiefs, and towels, as well as armloads of dresses from which to choose the ones I'd wear that day. The black? Or the black? Possibly the black. We were in mourning, but all of the dresses, being Rose Bertin's handiwork, were of the most exquisite fabric and cut.

My windows slightly open and facing south—even the mildest breeze carried with it the smell of orange blossoms. Southern light, light from the Midi, turning the crystal facets of my chandeliers to honey. I was the Queen of France! The Queen of France, bathing her soft white body (chastely hidden under a flannel gown) in her swan-shaped tub on wheels. The Queen of France donning her taffeta wrapper and dimity slippers, before returning to bed for a breakfast cup of chocolate and a breakfast roll, Eggplant curled adoringly at her feet.

Then the door leading to the Salon of the Nobles would fly open (letting in a faint whiff of stink from those endless unlit hallways where the lowest of the low tunneled their invisible way throughout the chateau) and the parade would begin. Abbé Vermond with some tiresome piece of state business, or occasionally a letter from my mother. "Madame my dear daughter"—for so she addressed me—"They say one cannot tell the Queen from the Princes, that they are shockingly familiar with you . . ." And who might be this *they* who told her that? None other than Count Florimund Mercy d'Argentau, blabbermouth Austrian envoy to the court, planted there by Madame my dear mother, and otherwise known as Mercy.

Next my two brothers-in-law, the so-called familiar Princes of the Blood, fat pedantic Provence, and elegant witty Artois (whose observation that there was only one King of France, and that was the Queen, Mercy couldn't let slip to my mother fast enough), followed by the little Princesse de Lamballe, a pretty but not especially bright widow of two and twenty, who would wring her unnaturally gigantic hands and burst into tears at the least provocation, a trait I willfully mistook for warmheartedness, so eager was I to have a girlfriend more or less my own age. All of them sitting there watching me drink my chocolate and eat my roll, Vermond stiffly, Provence hungrily, Artois somewhat salaciously, as the Princesse de Lamballe discreetly blew her nose. A tableau I often found myself studying in the immense mirror on the opposing wall, where all of us appeared ludicrously small in comparison to the furniture, like dolls made to live in the wrong size dollhouse.

At some point the toilet table would be rolled in and the Grande Toilette would commence, during which Monsieur Léonard would do my hair while a crowd of high court officials, including those ill-dressed hags pushing forty I'd made the mistake of referring to as "bundles," looked on, their panniers mashed together. Initially they came to ooh and aah and garner fashion tips, but eventually, I'm sorry to say, their chief objective was to compile evidence against me, and not just (as I thought) because I was so much better looking, even with my hair in curling papers, but also (as my mother had to keep on reminding me) because I was Austrian.

As if marrying Louis could undo centuries of enmity between our two countries. As if I had always been, was, and would always be Antonia, never Antoinette. As if on the stroke of twelve I could remove my face the way I'd remove my mask at a ball, revealing my true monstrous aspect.

Or, as the pamphleteers wrote:

> Little Queen of twenty-one,
> If you don't stop making fun,
> We'll kick you straight back home.

After Léonard took off the curling papers, he frizzed my hair with a hot iron, combed it out with nettle juice, powdered it with bean flour, then mounted a ladder in order to affix the horsehair cushion that would form an armature for the final hairdo.

Cypresses and black marigolds and wheat sheaves and fruit-filled cornucopias—a hairdo reminding everyone that while they mourned the loss of one King, they also looked forward to the bounty the next would bring. Or how about the Inoculation Hairdo, commemorating the Princes' victory over smallpox? One day Léonard made me Minerva. One day he made me an English garden with lawns, hills, and streams. One day he made me the world.

Really, you could put anything on your head your head your head . . . so long as it didn't (excuse me) snap your neck.

Léonard used long steel pins to hold the cushion in place and combed my own hair up over it. Then he matted everything down with pomade, creating a kind of moist hive under which fleas and lice bred, and soon enough there wasn't a fashionable lady alive who wasn't using a long thin stick identical to the one Léonard made for me, complete with a little ivory claw, to scratch away at her scalp like mad.

Whatever I did, everyone wanted to do; whatever I wore, everyone coveted. First they wanted to copy me, then they began to hate me.

But, *comme on dit*, one must suffer to be beautiful.

It took forever, the royal *lever*.

By the time Louis got there he'd have been up for hours, hammering away on his forge, shooting at cats, or watching the arriving guests through his telescope. My poor dear Louis, squinting his pale blue nearsighted eyes in an effort to locate me within that thicket of courtiers and under that mountain of hair. Smiling with delight when he finally did, while attempting to appear cool and detached.

"Bonjour, la Reine," he would say. Never one for nicknames or wordplay of any sort, my Lou-Lou, drawing up his chair, companionable. After our initial awkwardness, once we got the fact out of the way that two people couldn't possibly have less in common than a reclusive locksmith and his impudent wife, we actually became quite close, more or less along the lines of Aphrodite and Hephaestus. Just as the pamphleteers would later suggest, aiming merely to hurt but nonetheless hitting the target, in that vexing way that cruelty can sometimes approximate truth.

So sweet, my Louis. What was he doing in that nest of vipers?

"I had a dream," I recall him once confiding. "It was in another century, but the doors opened and shut the same way."

February. Low gray skies and a dusting of snow. Snow disturbed by the carriage wheels, like bean flour in a draft. The Archduke rides with his head hanging out the window and his mouth open, catching snowflakes on his tongue. Both he and his sister adore snow and always have. When Antoinette was a little girl she told him she was made of snow, and he couldn't sleep, terrified that he'd come into her room in the morning and find nothing but a puddle.

Definitely not cute, the Archduke Maximilian— slow, rather, and grossly fat, as well as harelipped and given to "smudging" his consonants—though that's hardly reason for the Princes of the Blood to cut him, as they do. No sooner has he huffed and puffed his way up among the noisy stinking throng of courtiers and servants and messengers and sedan chairs crowding the Queen's Staircase, barely escaped the humiliation of walking smack into a *trompe l'oeil* vista at the head of the stairs, negotiated the narrow corridor that gives through an arcaded opening onto the Room of the Queen's Guard, made his way past the series of ornate gilt-painted doors that lead from the Queen's Antechamber to the Salon of the Nobles and into the Queen's Bedchamber, than Provence and Artois have hightailed it out the door at the rear of the bedroom, into the Salon of Peace and thence through the Hall of Mirrors (a million ungainly Provences, a million handsome Artoises) to the King's Bedchamber, where they collapse on a sofa in its winter upholstery of thick red velvet embroidered with over a hundred and twenty pounds of gold thread and break out laughing.

According to protocol, the Princes of the Blood are supposed to call on the Archduke, not the other way around. Certainly they aren't supposed to lead the Archduke a merry chase.

But is it Antoinette's naivete that permits her to trivialize the incident? Or is it, rather, her disdain for whatever it is in the French character that finds such protocol of vital importance? In fact the Princes are engaging in a political act that is openly hostile, but Antoinette is more interested in the steady accumulation of the snow, the way it's making the conical topiary on the Southern Terrace look like the little wooden trees in the manger scene she used to be allowed to play with at Christmas, before she took the Baby Jesus off to her room and lost it. The snow is turning the parterre's dark green love knots white and piling up on the heads of the statues, making them look like bewigged courtiers rather than Greek gods and goddesses.

Tomorrow is Valentine's Day. Antoinette's heart beats faster, though she has no one in mind, or maybe someone, but no one in particular. They'll ride out in a sledge, she and Maxie, just like when they were children. Later, boiled chicken, a potato. He isn't clever enough for cards, but maybe the Princesse de Guéménée can be persuaded to read his fortune. A little adventure, a little romance? A rendezvous at shepherd's hour with a mysterious dark-haired woman?

Not likely, given the harelip.

Snow falling softly, softly. Snow covering the 11,520 black and white paving stones of the Marble Court, where carriage traffic is strictly forbidden. Snow falling on the 250 carriages waiting in the Forward Court for their owners, and on the hatless head of the kitchen gardener's third assistant's lackey, waiting against an espaliered fruit tree for the arrival of Françoise, with whom he has been having a little dalliance, though tonight he will wait and wait, growing more and more furious to have been jilted on Valentine's Eve, without realizing that meanwhile Françoise is watching the first macule erupt on her pretty forehead and does not need her cards read to know she's doomed.

How late it is getting! The snow still falling though lighter now, little flakes through air made wet and fresh by the storm, an oddly pale lucent darkness. And footprints everywhere, up and down the Stairways of the Hundred Steps, along the Infants' Walk as far as the Neptune Fountain, in and out of the bosquet at the Baths of Apollo, and around and around Air, Water, Earth, and Fire; Spring, Summer, Winter, Fall. Footprints of messengers and courtiers, lovers and thieves. Rabbits and deer. Murderers. Foxes.

Notwithstanding which, the gilt-grilled doors surrounding the Marble Court, like all the doors at Versailles, are unlocked. Ironic, when you think about it, given the King's favorite pastime, though clearly he considers the locks he makes not so much safety devices as intriguing puzzles. In fact the mechanism of the locks themselves is still fairly primitive; protection is provided by elaborate warding, or the addition of secret shutters to hide the keyholes, or sometimes even imposter keyholes.

Besides, once you're inside the chateau you can go practically anywhere, assuming you don't get caught in a traffic jam of sedan chairs, or, having wended your way through the insane maze of corridors honeycombing the Nobles' Wing, landed in some airless hopeless squalid cabinet of a room where you will live out the rest of your life entirely forgotten by everybody including your closest relatives. On the other hand you might find yourself remembered, plucked up and dressed like a soldier and sent to fight the enemy in some foreign land—Turkey, or America, or Spain. After which you might find yourself dead, consigned to a coffin that is, at least, bigger than the cabinet you lived in before . . .

And the King? Oh, the King has no need for doors. Just look at him, climbing the facade hand over hand like a big tame monkey, hauling himself across the stone balustrade and suddenly appearing in the Queen's Bed-chamber, scaring her half to death.

THE KING'S PENIS

The curtains part, revealing the Queen's Bedchamber; the bed curtains part, revealing the Queen. Elegant, coquettish, in charming disarray, she is seated on the right side of the bed, facing the audience. On her lap, Eggplant, a pug; to her left, Louis XVI, King of France, a softly snoring lump. It is the middle of the night—perhaps three o'clock. Though there is no moon, the room is eerily lit by recently fallen snow.

ANTOINETTE, *speaking to the lump in the overwrought high-pitched "voice" of Eggplant, whom she's hoisted by his underarms and holds in front of her face:* Ah! Mon Dieu! What is to be done with the Queen? She is incorrigible. When she isn't tearing around on horseback like an Amazon, she's at the races, rubbing shoulders with harlots. And really, who's to say which is which, Queen or harlot? Are those diamonds genuine or paste? It's so hard to tell these days. It's so hard to tell whose big blue eyes those are, riveted on the flies of all the handsome young men.

The lump suddenly sits up and speaks. Antoinette!

ANTOINETTE, *still speaking through Eggplant:* The King is awake. *She returns the pug to her lap and leans over to give Louis a peck on the cheek.* And did the King have pleasant dreams?

LOUIS: I don't know.

ANTOINETTE: Let us see. *She lifts the blankets, peers underneath, then sits back up.* Apparently.

LOUIS: I want a look, too. *He takes a quick peek and ducks his head, embarrassed.*

ANTOINETTE: One can only hope the King was dreaming of the Queen.

LOUIS, *petulant:* I don't know, I told you. *Pause, thinking.* I seem to remember I was making you a spinning wheel.

ANTOINETTE: But you actually did that, Lou-Lou, remember? You did make me a spinning wheel. *She sets Eggplant off to one side, then shifts position, leaning back into the pillows and opening her arms.* Only let's not think about that now. Let's only think about pleasant things. Come here. Come give us a kiss.

LOUIS: But the spinning wheel *is* a pleasant thing.

ANTOINETTE: Of course it is, my treasure. Of course it is.

They both disappear under the bedclothes. There is a pe-

riod of agitated movement; a hand appears, a foot. A final
spasm; Eggplant jumps to the floor.

Louis, *from under the covers:* Owww!

Antoinette: Let me see if I can . . .

Louis: No. Please.

Antoinette: . . . just pry this back a . . .

Louis: STOP IT!!!

*They both emerge from under the covers, Louis red-faced
and panting slightly, Antoinette with tears running down her
cheeks. Throughout the scene the room has been growing
lighter—the pale light of a winter morning. Sounds of footsteps, doors being knocked on with knuckles or delicately
scratched at with the little fingernail, muffled voices, doors
opening—the Queen's household includes more than five
hundred officers and servants, early risers, all of them. It is
now possible to see the gilt balustrade fencing off the Queen's
bed and its occupants from the rest of the room, where a large
crowd will soon assemble, eager to watch the royal pair eat
their breakfast, the male and female of the species in their
natural habitat.*

Antoinette: But there's so little time before the
multitudes descend. Maybe if you ate less? Doctor
Lassone seems to think that might help. Last night
you ate a whole roast piglet. Don't pretend you
didn't—I was watching. Also those pastries. Or
maybe if you agreed to let him make the incision?

Louis: You didn't see the instruments. He showed

me his instruments. *Hiding his eyes, shuddering.* I don't like to think about it.

ANTOINETTE: Well then, think about this. Think about what will become of us if we can't produce an heir to the throne, and meanwhile that wretched cross-eyed midget who is married to your brother produces offspring like a rabbit. What then?

LOUIS: I wish you wouldn't talk about the Comtesse d'Artois like that. She can't help the way she looks.

ANTOINETTE: Of course she can't. She's Sardinian. *Yawning.* But if we're not going to create an heir this morning, then let me sleep. I was up till all hours, trying to win my money back from the Marquis de Conflans, that rotten crook.

LOUIS: *Yawns noisily, stretches, and leaps from the bed.* The Queen's wish is my command.

ANTOINETTE: Well then . . . *She stares pointedly at the King's erection, tenting the cloth of the royal nightshirt, then makes a pair of scissors of her fingers and holds them aloft.* Snip snip. *Suiting the action to the words.* Snip snip.

LOUIS: Don't tease.

Antoinette sighs and pulls the blankets over her head.

LOUIS: Besides, it's not just me. It wouldn't hurt for you to get more sleep, Lassone says.

ANTOINETTE, *her voice muffled, from under the covers:*

Ah. I see. All I need to do to become pregnant is get more sleep.

LOUIS: Only another hour or so each night, Lassone says. And less wine, though that hardly makes sense, since you don't take wine to begin with. *He cocks his head, listening.* They're coming. Oh, that's so bad, so bad! The tub wheels should be oiled—I can hear them squeaking all the way from here.

ANTOINETTE, *still muffled:* I suppose I could start drinking wine, in order to give it up. Just like my sister Carlotta would always give up liver pudding for Lent. *She laughs, sticks out her head.* I know! Let's put talking pâtés on our pillows, like in "La Belle Eulalie." Then we could escape and no one would know the difference. We could go to Paris, Lou-Lou! We could have fun!

LOUIS: We could have fun. *Suddenly cheerful.* I could oil those wheels!

STAIRCASE OF
THE AMBASSADORS

Fifty-eight steps from the centermost of the three gilt-grilled front doors, across the vestibule's rose-colored marble pavement and around a phalanx of dark squat piers supporting a dark low ceiling, to the foot of the staircase. Purposely oppressive, the vestibule—echoey, claustrophobic. "On thy belly shalt thou crawl," the overriding message.

And then suddenly at the foot of the staircase the whole thing opens wide, like breath expelled after passing a graveyard. The infinite pours in through a massive skylight three stories up.

No one standing there can resist looking into the face of God, which is to say into the sun. The Doge of Genoa, bringing the Sun King a coffer of precious jewels. The Duc de Nevers, imprisoned by the Sun King for baptizing a pig. Jean Racine, suspected by the Sun King of being a poisoner. The Earl of Portland, hoping to convince the Sun King to drive James II as far from England as possible. Bonne, Ponne, and Nonne, the Sun King's hyperactive water spaniels. Dr. Guy-Crescent Fagon with his frightening tools, to let the Sun King's blood.

Ghosts, all of them. The Staircase of the Ambassadors is no longer there — hasn't been since 1752, when Louis XV ordered it destroyed to make apartments for Adélaïde. It was falling apart, anyway, he claimed: the cast-bronze structure supporting the skylight was beginning to wobble, and rain was beginning to leak through. An ill-advised decision for posterity, though certainly not surprising from the same man who remarked, *"Après moi, le déluge."*

In any case, ghosts are often associated with stairways, liking to hover at their head, or to drag noisy things such as chains up and down them. And don't stairways provide an avenue of connection between two levels or, really, worlds?

For instance, there by the fountain on the landing, where the two flights of stairs branch out, one to the right, one to the left. Isn't that La Voisin, in her trim white cap, with her bag of arsenic and nail cuttings, powdered crayfish and Spanish fly? La Voisin the Sorceress, who helps the women of the Sun King's court — many of them the Sun King's past, present, or future mistresses

—obtain bigger whiter breasts, or smaller whiter hands.

It's difficult to tell for sure, since the Staircase is teeming with people who turn out on closer inspection to be unreal. The conquistador, fur trapper, and two red Indians in nothing but loincloths, gathered together on a loggia above the left-branching flight of stairs? The work of Charles Le Brun, master illusionist. Probably the only place at Versailles where you'd find a live red Indian would be out past the Grand Canal, in the zoo.

Nor would you be likely to run into the Bedouin prince and African tribal chief who stand in rapt discourse on a facing loggia.

Even the loggias themselves aren't real, nor are the oriental rugs draped over their parapets, no matter how temptingly soft to the touch they appear to be. The rugs are there to support the idea that this is a festival day, the Sun King having returned triumphant from the Dutch War, meaning —*grâce à Dieu!*— he will once again be able to line the walkways with tulips, his favorite flower.

A festival day, and not only have people from the four corners of the earth joined to receive the King, but also, in a mixed metaphor of hyperbolic proportion, all the divinities of Parnassus. Clio and Polyhymnia, Hercules and Minerva. Calliope, Thalia, Apollo. Fame and Mercury, Magnificence and Pegasus. Authority, Strength, and Vigilance. Also the twelve months of the year, back in the good old days when they were still named for gods and goddesses. Also a great variety of exotic birds—peacocks, ibises, and so on.

Not to mention *actual* people, many of them the Sun King's mistresses, since, let's face it, the King of France is expected to be excessively virile, a lion among men.

Up the stairs and down the stairs, delicately lifting their skirts to avoid an unsightly tumble. Beautiful but stupid Mademoiselle de Fontanges in her turquoise-blue riding habit. Mademoiselle de la Vallière and her cunning daughter, Marie, the two of them in matching black velvet gowns. Madame de Maintenon, otherwise known as Your Solidity. Madame de Montespan in all of her many incarnations, young and slender, old and fat, but always with that infuriating parrot jabbering away on her shoulder.

Up and down, up and down.

Let us walk among the tulips! Dance until dawn! Spin the roulette wheel! Slip the King a love philter when he isn't paying attention! Look at me! No, me!

Watch out, though. Sometimes La Voisin's clients get more than they bargain for. Sometimes out pops the Devil, with his sharp little hooves and his appetite for discord.

Nor do you want to get so involved in the spectacle that you fail to notice the python on the ceiling, lying dead at Apollo's feet. "His Majesty," as the *Mercure Galant* explains, "putting a stop to the secret rebellions His enemies have tried starting, as depicted by the serpent Python who originates from the gross impurities of the earth . . ."

$\nearrow$ Presently, the girl takes a walk. So many doors to choose among, so many people. Stupid, witty, amorous, bored, dark-eyed, washed-out, plucked-lipped, hairy. Scratch scratch scratch, with the little fingernail.

"Come in, my dear."

"Hello, grandmother."

Dancing, billiards, reversi, roulette. The path of the pins or the path of the needles. Sorbet, asparagus, cock kidneys, bonbons. Sausage, pigeon eggs, truffles, lemonade.

So the girl eats what's put before her, and all of a sudden there's a dear little tabby cat sitting at her feet, going *meow meow how could you do it?* Meaning how could she ever have managed to swallow a single bite, the wolf having gotten there first and carved her granny up into dinner.

But did I say *girl*? What I meant was woman. Queen,

actually. When I said girl I meant Queen of France.

Then the wolf says in a serious tone, "Undress and get in bed with me."

I admit, I was credulous. I admit I played too much roulette, cavagnole, lansquenet. The word most often used in describing me was "pleasure," as in "Antoinette lives for pleasure."

Will a lion roar in the forest, when he hath no prey? Will a young lion cry out of his den, if he hath taken nothing?

I think I was casting about among the millions of things I was surrounded with to find just one, JUST ONE LITTLE THING that would somehow stand for the whole. One thing to fix my eyes on, to still my racing heart. A silver snuffbox such as got stolen daily by the hot-fingered riffraff the place was full of? A diamond bracelet? An especially fine apricot?

God knows I was nice enough, kind enough. (I *was*, too.)

God knows it drove me mad to watch my cross-eyed sister-in-law's belly get bigger and bigger, in preparation for the day not so very far off when she'd spread her legs and out would pop the Duc d'Angoulême.

And meanwhile in the Orangerie the potted trees put forth their sweet white blossoms. And meanwhile my husband kept shooting and hammering and forging; I kept piling more and more feathers on my head. Trying to redress some imbalance, I suppose, like the spurned lover who turns to opiates or chocolate or drink.

It was the fashion, then, to complain about everything. It was the fashion to say, "Oh, if only I were in Paris," unless that's where you happened to be, in which case you'd say, "Oh, if only I were at Versailles." Whereas meanwhile I lived for pleasure.

For example, my "lovers." Count Esterházy, with his sly Magyar eyes, who shot bread pellets at me when I was laid low with measles. The Prince de Ligne, who told me my soul was as beautiful and white as my face. Women, too. I was to have had unnatural relations with women, wild orgies at night under the stars while my husband slept the deep sleep of the innocent. My wedding ring disappeared, and it was whispered that it had been stolen by a witch from the Massif Central. To keep me barren, it was whispered—as if supernatural forces were actually required for such a thing.

"Where shall I put my petticoat?" the girl asks the wolf. "Where shall I put my stockings?"

"Throw them on the fire, dear. You won't need them anymore."

Though who knows how these things happen? Maybe there *was* witchcraft at work, only not on my womb. Maybe witchcraft was behind the previous summer's crop failures, which led to the following winter's grain shortage, which led to the flour wars of May. The same year my cross-eyed sister-in-law prepared to give birth, and a fortune was being poured into Rheims Cathedral to refurbish it for my husband's coronation. Seamstresses busy stitching gold fleurs-de-lis on everything in sight. Cobblers busy making the violet boots with high red heels in which my husband would totter toward the altar. Bird catchers busy catching the hundreds of birds that would be let loose to beat their poor wings against the vaulted arches, as the Archbishop of Rheims tipped the Holy Ampulla full of coronation oil over my husband's head. "May the King possess the strength of a rhinoceros. May he drive the nations of our enemies before him like a rushing wind."

Because, really, who knows why it never rained during the summer of 1774? Why the soil turned to dust and when the rain finally came, the worm got into the bud? Shall a trumpet be blown in the city, and the people not be afraid? Shall there be evil in a city, and the Lord hath not done it? You might just as well say a witch put a spell on the sky.

I admit, I was oblivious. I liked to go to the races with my charming brother-in-law, playfully dispute the merits of Glowworm, King Pepin. Who knows why one horse triumphed, another came up lame? I liked to watch the little silver ball in the roulette wheel leap from number to number like a flea.

And on that May morning when a crowd of peasants poured through the gates at the Place d'Armes, filling the Forward Court with their furious voices and pale up-turned faces, with their rumbling stomachs and loaves of moldy bread, who knows why I didn't see among them the invisible hand of the future, wielding a bloody knife?

It wasn't because I was too stupid. It wasn't even because I was unwilling to face facts. No, it was because I was completely uninterested in food—always had been, always would be—and off somewhere else, sequestered as usual, no doubt taking a walk. Alone for a change, alone and thinking things over. The happy days of my childhood and the gardens of Schönbrunn, the way the sweet woodruff grew thickly around the base of each shade tree in a collar of lace. May wine, Carlotta told me, this is what's used to flavor May wine, and she picked a flower and made me taste it, but it was so bitter I had to spit it out. There was still snow on the mountains; our mother galloped past us on her favorite stallion, seated astride like a man. Calling out in her wild imperious way, *Guten Morgen, meine Schatzerl!*, the sound of hoofbeats continuing to thud behind her long after she was gone. How warm the air, yet with a smell like melted snow. Carlotta put her arms around me and laughed. Inside my body, my soul stirred. Changeless, changeless, as if that could compensate for all the rest.

"Oh, grandmother! What big teeth you have!"

"Oh, grandmother! What big—"

Presently the Queen takes a walk.

Around the Latona Fountain, where the stone frogs perch with their poor sad mouths eternally wide open, hoping against hope for a drink that never comes, and then across the bright springy turf of the Tapis Vert and toward the Grand Canal.

There was the smell of newly cut grass and boxwood, the sun at my back, pleasantly warm and the canal extending before me like a blue sparkling avenue all the way to a place where a person might fall off the edge of the world if she wasn't paying attention, which, I admit, I wasn't. Woodsmen were busy chopping the trees that hadn't made it through the previous winter, talking to each other in that easy way of the peasant class, making jokes, singing, until they saw me approach and clammed up, growing busier than ever. In those days I think I was still more admired than despised, though perhaps also (unbeknownst to me) pitied a little, pity being the prelude to contempt.

"Bonjour," I said, and came to a halt near one particularly industrious pair of broad-shouldered youths. *"Comment ça va?"* I inquired, whereupon in keeping with

the protocol they threw themselves obediently, if not a trifle clownishly, at my feet. The smell of sap, of wood chips and sweat and the sweet May breeze, combined with some oddly exhilarating aroma the canal was giving off, a mix of algae and trout spawn, was going to my head. "Please get up," I said, knowing that as they did they couldn't fail to catch a glimpse of slim white ankle. Even the Queen of France should be allowed to forgo her stockings on a warm spring day.

I know what you're thinking. But NO NO NO! — I would never be untrue to Louis, though I'm also willing to admit I liked to flirt, especially if the man had a long humorous mouth and clear blue eyes like the taller of the two, and so I made a joke of my own at the expense of our current Finance Minister, Turgot, a sort of rude play on words involving *impotence* and the single property tax, or *impôt unique*, he'd recently instated.

"It's a bad idea," the shorter of the two young men said. His eyebrows ran together over the bridge of his nose, giving him a grave, unforgiving look. "God's will, not the farmer's lack of it, is behind a poor harvest. The rich merchant buys what little grain there is and makes the baker pay for it through the nose, and then the baker turns around and charges the hungry woodcutter an arm and a leg for a single lousy loaf crawling with bugs."

"No worse than that icebreaker," replied Blue Eyes,

referring to Minister Turgot's machine, an ill-starred contraption that not only failed to break up the floes at the head of the Seine the previous February, but also was said to have capsized in a tantrum of whirling impedimenta, taking several of its operators down with it.

"The machine was only responsible for three deaths," said Eyebrows. "The tax will starve thousands."

"Turgot won't last," I said. "I am sure of it. Even now, wakened by the spring sun, the wheat anticipates the thresher's blade."

I could see the new leaves on the beech trees, pricked and moving this way and that like the ears of animals. Listening, listening . . . What is the Queen saying? What impropriety is she committing? The sun had gone behind a large dark cloud; the wind was picking up.

"And then?" said Eyebrows, lifting his axe, clearly impatient with the conversation and ready to get back to work.

"And then we shall have someone even worse," said Blue Eyes, grinning sardonically.

Suddenly a gentle rain began to fall, dotting the canal with millions of tiny bright eruptions, like flung pearls. On my cheeks and eyelashes, my ungloved hands, my uncoiffed head—for a moment I stood there, face uptilted and open-mouthed like one of Latona's frogs, and then all at once the sky filled with millions of tiny bright birds, beating their wings like mad to outrace the approaching storm, and for some reason I felt extremely happy.

"Your Majesty should find shelter," Eyebrows said, his gaze fixed on his axe blade, which he was in the process of sharpening with a whetstone. "Your Majesty might take a chill."

Blue Eyes bent to retrieve his own axe, and it occurred to me that he was trying to hide his amusement. The three of us were, after all, more or less the same age, and I was clearly in excellent health—had circumstances been different we'd no doubt have linked arms and run laughing into the beech grove. Though maybe he, too, had grown bored with the conversation. Maybe he wanted me to leave so that he could relinquish all pretense of continuing to work in what had by now become a fairly steady downpour.

"In any case," I said, "I had better get back to the chateau. The King will be looking for me."

Except of course he wasn't; he was off hunting in the densely wooded area somewhere near the Pond of the Iron Nail, and returned, as I did, drenched to the skin. "Got one," he told me, simultaneously making a note of the fact in his diary, but one *what*, I never had a clue.

Meanwhile the Prince de Poix, supported by the royal guards, had managed to disperse the angry mob, promising them good quality bread at two *sous* a loaf. Shortly thereafter the rain stopped, as quickly as it had started. I changed into Masked Desire, my latest Rose Bertin creation, and traded gossip with the Princesse de Lamballe (always an uneven exchange, given her fundamental aversion to speak ill of anyone, living or dead), and, more gratifyingly, with Artois, who told me the so-called inedible loaves wielded by the mob had in fact been cut open earlier and painted green and black, to make them look moldy. I played the harp; I did some needlework. I dined indifferently on the first asparagus of the season, likewise the first *fraises des bois*, cunningly baked into tarts shaped like hearts, diamonds, spades, clubs, each berry no bigger than my baby fingernail. I made eyes at this man, that man. I triumphed at roulette. Eventually I went to bed.

Can a bird fall in a snare upon the earth, where no gin is for him? Shall one take up a snare from the earth and shall have nothing in it?

Shh! Shh! Blow out the candles, offer a prayer. The body of the Queen of France is tossing and turning on her bed of needles and pins.

The body of the Queen of France, tossing and turning, and there deep inside her, what?

Lights and liver? Bones and blood?

No. The body of the Queen of France and there deep

inside her the soul: the girl, taking a walk. From the gardens of Schönbrunn to the Grand Canal of Versailles; from the taste of sweet woodruff to the smell of rain and fish. A straight line connecting the two prime coordinates that, if only she'd paid better attention to her studies, she could have used to locate the third, without which her life would always lack dimension.

Every life has a shape. Even the lives of dogs, though they're born embodying theirs, unlike humans. Even Eggplant, his big round eyeballs rolling from side to side under his silky eyelids, snoring and twitching and dreaming at the foot of the bed. Even a sparrow, a trout, a flea.

Of course death is never a coordinate, not for humans at least.

Which is why it's wrong to say that a life gets cut short.

Turgot's Lament
(after Purcell)

Thy will, oh False One, has betrayed me,
My power revoked at thy behest.
More I would, but cannot save thee
From thy cruel extravagance.

When I am laid in earth
May my words create
Desolation in thy breast.
Forget me, ah! while I enjoy thy fate.

COUNT FALKENSTEIN

A spring evening, 1777. Jeanne Bécu Du Barry's estate at Lou-
veciennes. The moon is full and a light breeze is blowing. A
perfect evening, in other words, were it not for the fact that the
French economy is growing weaker by the minute, war is
brewing in the Low Countries, and the King and Queen still
haven't managed to consummate their marriage. The
Queen's eldest brother, Joseph, recently arrived in Paris, is
paying Madame Du Barry a visit. He's traveling incognito (in
the guise of "Count Falkenstein"), liking to view himself as a
cloak-wrapped stranger who appears from out of nowhere,
performs good deeds, and only later is revealed to be Holy
Roman Emperor. When the curtain rises Joseph can be seen
looking out an open window, stage left, moonlight illuminat-
ing the serious expression on his face. He's wearing a toupee,
and what's left of his own hair is in a long pigtail down his
back; his eyes are protuberant, not unlike Eggplant's. Jeanne
meanwhile reclines on a striped sofa, center stage. As buxom
as her guest is rake-thin, she is bursting from a flowered

dressing gown and has her hands literally full, eating a roast chicken.

JOSEPH: I tried reasoning with him. With both of them. It's like talking to a wall.

JEANNE, *chewing*: What did you say?

JOSEPH: That he has to have the operation. That their lives depend on producing an heir. His moronic brother, Artois, already has two, you know, and a third on the way. Also, she has to stop gambling. Gambling and flirting. Her debts come to almost five hundred thousand *livres*.

JEANNE: Does she love him?

JOSEPH: I don't know. Mercy told my mother she's got the King wrapped around her little finger. She's more like a mistress than a wife, he says.

JEANNE: You could do worse, believe me.

JOSEPH: I'm sorry. I didn't mean—

JEANNE: Please. Sit down. You're making me nervous. *She rings a bell and her page appears, in his pink suit and snow white turban.* Another bottle of champagne, Zamor, but this time it should be a whole lot colder. Ice-cold, my pet. Do you understand what I mean by that?

ZAMOR: Yes, Madame. *He bows and exits, stage right.*

JEANNE: He doesn't have a clue, but he's so nice to look at.

Joseph begins pacing back and forth behind the sofa; Jeanne continues to devour the chicken, thoughtful, licking her fingers.

JEANNE: By the way, I think you're wrong.

JOSEPH: What?

JEANNE: About the operation. Wrong. Even if she loves him, which I don't think she does. Louis doesn't want to be King any more than your sister wants to be Queen. But once they produce an heir that'll be that—there'll be no turning back.

JOSEPH: You're joking.

JEANNE: I have no sense of humor, haven't you heard?

JOSEPH: And what do you suggest they do with the crown?

JEANNE: That's easy. Give it to someone else. Give it to Provence. Provence has had his eye on the crown since the day he was born. He's a bully. A pig. He'll make a wonderful King.

Joseph leaves the window and walks over to sit beside Jeanne.

JOSEPH: Even if I thought you were right, which I don't, I'd still have to try convincing Louis to have the operation. I promised my mother.

JEANNE, *taking a last bite of the chicken, then turning to kiss him:* Such a good little boy . . .

JOSEPH: The operation. The Queen's behavior. The
alliance with Austria. Three things. I promised.

JEANNE: Shhh. Come here.

JOSEPH: Her final request, really.

JEANNE: Aren't you being a little melodramatic?

THE CHAMBER OF
THE PENDULUM CLOCK

Tick tick tick tick. Twenty-two kilometers from Paris to Versailles. The season changing, the summer ending. August of Wheat, August of Oats. Deepening shadows, violet, indigo. The mill wheels turn, the mice move indoors.

Six hundred steps from the court to the entrance, fifty-eight steps from the door to the stairs. Tap tap tap tap. Shoes of soft leather, hard diamond heels. Where is the time gone? Who is the thief?

Where is the farmer who marks its passage, in hours long as the harvest allows? Mown fields unspool like bolts of dark velvet, snipped short at nightfall, rolled up and stored. The cat goes out hunting, the soul shuts its doors.

Transfiguration, the Feast of the Virgin. From Whitsun to All Saints', two hundred days. Down the long hallway, then left at the windows. Dice flung, a curse, in the chamber of clocks.

The Queen has grown restless. The Queen wants distraction. She's tired of sitting alone in her room, embroidering purses. Silk purse from a sow's ear, meaning the King. My dear, says Artois, what a pleasant surprise. Licking his lips as he scoops up the dice.

Tick tick tick tick. Shadows like water, flickering candles. The Clockmaker fixes the stars in their courses, planets and moons, a ruby, a pearl. From Easter to Whitsun, from All Saints' to Advent. From Advent to Christmas to darkest despair. The Baby's grown up, the Baby is dying, the Baby can't wait to be born once again.

Far far away in her garden retreat, the Queen's mother sits like a sack of sand. Snow on the mountaintops, eternal snow, her son in Bavaria, waging war. How old she's grown, old and ugly. France fighting England, no heir yet in sight. *Madame my dear daughter, be prudent, take care.* You might as well caution the sun not to rise. The King of Prussia rattles his saber, one eye on Austria, one eye on France.

In the chamber of clocks the gamblers play on. Clock of Creation, Clock of the Sphere. The Queen flings the dice across the green felt. A minute cracks open, a second comes out. Tiny, a bubble, its walls thin as hope.

$\overline{}$ And what *is* pleasure, really? If I lived for pleasure, what does that mean?

A lesser god than Eros, certainly. Not even a god, when you come to think about it. A kobold. An imp.

Louis finally consented to the operation, following my brother's visit. Early September, the time of the grape harvest, just before the Blessed Virgin's birthday. One little snip of Lassone's knife, that was all it took, and the next thing I knew the marriage was consummated. In the meantime Louis had a secret passage built between our two bedrooms, so he could tunnel his way through to me like an ardent mole, without attracting the attention of the well-wishers and curiosity-seekers hanging out in the Bull's Eye Chamber at all hours of the day and night.

"I am experiencing the most important happiness of my entire life," I wrote to tell my mother.

But pleasure?

In the absence of any impediment, I am sorry to say

that my husband's caresses grew a trifle distant, rushed, even. Before, he'd worked so hard to drum up enthusiasm for the task at hand; now he pumped away with the same sort of frenzied single-mindedness I'd seen him use operating the bellows. An abstracted expression on his face, his mind elsewhere, imagining the final product perhaps, a lock so magnificent it could defeat the Evil One himself. Not a great lover, Louis.

Of course, he had no practice. Just as, pamphleteers to the contrary, I had no basis of comparison. Antoinette and Louis, as inept in bed as on the throne, though goodness knows we tried. That mattress, those hands. The sound of his breathing, the weight of his torso. Just the two of us, two human bodies reduced to the place where the one had come into the other, nudging, nudging . . .

But did I feel stirred? Yes, I admit, I did, a little. It was like the way I'd sometimes feel while I was sitting for my portrait, an almost unendurable sense of my *self*, of the surfaces of Antoinette, her eyes trying not to blink, her lips growing more and more pursed and dry, her tongue dying to lick them. And then just when I'd think I couldn't bear to sit there like that one minute longer, I'd suddenly find myself on the outside looking in, a traveler in a carriage passing an apparently deserted house at nightfall. The windows dark, no hint of movement, yet somewhere deep inside, in the deepest darkest corner of the cellar, there would be a little sleeping animal who would prick up its ears.

Michaelmas came and went, then All Saints' Day, closely followed by All Souls'. I turned twenty-four; the peasants went into the woods with their baskets to harvest the acorns to fatten the pigs. The sweet damp smell of decaying oak leaves, brushfires burning, the first flakes of snow. My mother could no longer walk and had to be hauled up and down stairs on a green morocco sofa, operated by winches. "I hope the weather will be abominable," she wrote, "so the King won't get tired from hunting so much, and the Queen won't gamble every night into the small hours . . ." Christmastide, the Feast of the Innocents. For the New Year my husband gave me a pair of brilliant diamond earrings and a statue of cupid carving his bow from Hercules' club; the little moats around the Trianon, called fox jumps, froze. "I very much enjoy this pleasure," Louis confided to his aunts, meaning our newfound intimacy. "I am sorry to have been deprived of it for so long." In the hallways of Versailles everyone was sneezing and coughing and blowing his nose; in Paris Benjamin Franklin was a great hero, and all the women were wearing a coonskin hat called "The Insurgent" in his honor. "I have a bad toothache and a swollen face," my mother wrote, "even to the eyes, but no fever at all." We replaced Minister of Finance Turgot with Jacques Necker, a physiocrat with a prude, Carnival with Lent. Thin soup, boiled eggs, steamed fish, pottage. No dancing, no gambling; I had diarrhea.

Then it was spring; then I was pregnant.

Antoinette pregnant, imagine it! Just like the sows and the mares and the ewes and the nanny goats. The trees were budding, so girlish and fresh in their pale green shifts. I went to bed early and arose early; I went for long walks in the cool of the morning, amazed to see how precisely the world mirrored my condition. All the bulbs swelled and put forth pale green shoots. Hyacinth and narcissus—such names! As if some long dead botanist had been determined to keep us mindful of the wages of beauty. My waist grew four and a half *pouces* by Pentecost.

Nor was this pleasure, being devoid of any trace of the pain that makes pleasure possible. I had what I wanted and, for a moment at least, I was content. I ignored the rumors about the baby's patrimony; I knew they were false, which seemed sufficient reason to discount them. A great weakness in a Queen, you might say, such indifference to political nuance—no matter that it was based on a clear sense of my own moral rectitude. But evidently everyone was less interested in having a truly good Queen than in having a Queen who *appeared* good. So long as I feigned deference to even the silliest details of court etiquette, remembering for instance to send my dentist six dozen handkerchiefs a year, so long as I made a great show of enjoying the company of even the most tedious old bundles, stuck to a few boring hands of cavagnole, and turned in before midnight, I think I could have slept with every man in France.

I was content. Somnolent, dreamy. I imagined my baby, cradled in my arms. A beautiful baby, flawless, with blue eyes and that newborn smell of powder and milk. Sometimes a girl, but more usually a boy, because that was what was expected of me.

"Once you feel the child, you shouldn't sit or lie on chaises longues too much," wrote my mother, "except for an accident, *Gott behüte!*" So she must have taken pains to protect herself when she was carrying Joseph; by the time I came along she'd already given birth fourteen times and, aside from her need to dispense endless advice, was never exactly what you'd call maternal. Often eight or ten days would go by before I'd catch even the most fleeting glimpse of her, a giantess in chamois riding breeches and high-topped boots, closeted in her room with the Lord High Chamberlain and a mountain of paper. If I had a fever, it would be the court physician who'd lay a cold compress on my forehead; if I had a problem with my needlework, it would be one of the court tutors who'd unsnarl the yarn. As for the routine miseries of childhood, I wasn't allowed to have them. Hurt feelings? A bad dream? Stuff and nonsense. The only monster we had to fear was the King of Prussia.

Whereas I was resolved to be a perfect mother. A sound mind in a sound body, that would be me. I would go to bed early; I would finally read all those books Mercy had been pressing on me for years. I would breastfeed my baby, as Rousseau advised, rather than send him out to a wet nurse, and instead of swaddling him like a mummy, I would let him kick his little legs and shake his little arms as much as he wanted. On nice days I'd take him out in a wicker crib and show him the trees, the clouds, the sky. If he got frightened by the sound of hunting horns winding through the woods, I'd pick him up and kiss him. The King of Prussia might still be a monster, threatening war with Austria in retaliation for my brother Joseph's invasion of Lower Bavaria. Mercy might be warning me that if France refused to come to Austria's aid, it would kill my mother. And my husband might be reminding me that if it weren't for my brother's ambition, there wouldn't be a problem in the first place. Affairs of state, in other words, might require most of my attention, but the truth is, my heart was elsewhere.

Which maybe is what it means to be content: the heart safely secluded, a world unto itself.

Unlike being in the grip of Eros, who takes you over,

transporting you so thoroughly it's as if you have no heart, no head, no flesh even, every part of you burning in a single bright flame.

Unlike pleasure, which must be sought after.

The first time I felt the baby move I was walking through the Low Gallery with the strapping Princesse de Guéménée, her omnipresent pack of dogs, and the dainty flowerlike Madame Dillon. We were in those days still the best of friends, despite the fact that the Princesse's husband was madly in love with Madame Dillon, who was, herself, loyally devoted to him. It was late afternoon, the end of July; the sun was preparing to fall into the Atlantic Ocean hundreds of kilometers away to the west, bathing everything as far as the eye could see, trees and lawns and fountains and pools, in a molten red-gold light, as if the whole world were composed of a single red-gold substance.

"You'll want to establish a room for the baby here on the ground floor, adjacent to the terrace," announced the Princesse, speaking from her position as Governess to the Children of France. "That way, as soon as he is able, he'll take his first steps outdoors in the fresh air." She was a tall, rather badly made woman who, though pretty, maintained an unwavering look of deep concern, chiefly for the stupidity of others, and who claimed to communicate with the spirit world through her dogs.

"You seem so sure it will be a boy," said Madame Dillon. "I would predict a girl."

"Oh?" said the Princesse. "Why is that?"

"The way she carries."

"Antoinette is wide and flat through the hips. She has no alternative. Besides"—and here the Princesse indicated her dogs with a sweeping gesture—"I have it on the best authority. By next Christmas France will have the heir we've all been waiting for. A strong healthy baby boy, the reincarnation of Louis Quatorze himself."

We had come to a halt by one of the tall windows lining the Gallery; the light was no longer red-gold but red, and thin, almost watery, the way it gets when it prepares to fill with darkness. Lanterns hanging from the prows of the gondolas on the Grand Canal, lanterns circling Latona and her frogs, moving back and forth across the terraces, ferried by dark figures, men and women dressed for dancing and intrigue, mounting the steps between the Vases of the Sun.

Meanwhile the Princesse de Guéménée continued droning on and on. Clio, yap yap yap, animal magnetism, blah blah blah . . . "I still say it will be a girl," chimed in Madame Dillon. "You will be a girl, won't you?" she said, sweetly addressing my stomach, at which moment I felt the baby swim toward the surface like a fish about to leap from the water into the thin red air, as simultaneously a group of masked men and women burst through the doors from the Southern Terrace, bringing with them the combined smells of attar of roses, brandy, and perspiration. Racing together, laughing and chattering, their voices echoing off the smooth stone walls and the vaulted ceiling.

Pleasure-seekers, all of them.

The City of Sows, who can't be satisfied with noble loaves of barley and wheat but must have relishes and desserts. That's what Plato said.

Painting, embroidery, gold, ivory. Perfume, jewelry, courtesans, wine. Poets, rhapsodes, actors, choral dancers, beauticians, barbers, relish-makers, cooks.

Swineherds, too, to fatten the pigs so they'd be good to eat.

The City of Sows, the Feverish City. See them turning and turning on their golden spits, their fine skin cracking, releasing fat.

Whereas I was content. I was content for that one little moment as I stood by the tall window in the Low Gallery in the growing darkness, feeling my baby move inside me.

Speeches have a double form, the one true, the other false.

Plato also said that.

DUETTINO
(after Mozart)

MERCY (*entering the Bull's Eye Chamber through a door,*
stage right)

All is not lost yet;

We can still hope.

(*Antoinette enters stage left, humming to herself, the red vel-*
vet bag containing her missal over one arm.)

But here is the Queen; a golden opportunity.

I'll pretend not to see her.

(*Aside, loudly*)

If only she would come, that pearl of virtue,

Whose charms the King cannot resist.

ANTOINETTE (*aside, holding back*)

He's talking about me.

MERCY (*aside, to himself*)

After all, in this strange land

She's the best one can hope for.

Style means everything.

ANTOINETTE *(aside)*

> A spiteful tongue! Lucky for him
> He has my mother's blessing.

MERCY

> Bravo! Such discretion!
> And those modest eyes,
> That demure expression,
> Those . . .

ANTOINETTE *(aside)*

> Enough is enough.

(Both spring into motion, meeting at the door to the King's Bedchamber)

MERCY *(executing a deep, satiric bow)*

> After you,
> Your Royal Highness.

ANTOINETTE *(executing a low, satiric curtsy)*

> No, I insist,
> Most worthy sir.

MERCY

> No, you go first, pray.

ANTOINETTE

> No, no, after you.

MERCY AND ANTOINETTE *(together)*

> Your words can sway the King;
> Mine are like millet seed.

MERCY

> Expectant mother, first.

ANTOINETTE

First, brilliant statesman.

MERCY

Austria's pride and joy.

ANTOINETTE

The toast of France.

MERCY

Your comeliness.

ANTOINETTE

Your wine cellars.

MERCY

Your dramatic gifts.

ANTOINETTE

Your lies.

MERCY *(aside)*

I'll die of apoplexy

If I stay here one minute longer.

ANTOINETTE

Duplicitous old sodomite.

If only my mother knew . . .

(Exit Mercy in a fury.)

THE QUEEN'S
BEDCHAMBER

Almost a perfect cube, four *toises* wide, four long, four and a fraction high. A jewel box, the ideal receptacle in which to put a Queen, beginning with stumpy little Marie-Thérèse of Spain, the Sun King's long-suffering bride, who enjoyed the company of puppies and dwarfs, and whose teeth were black from eating chocolate. Queen-in-a-box. Open the lid and out she pops!

The Queen's apartments are to the left of the Marble Court, the King's to the right, both occupying more or less the same amount of floor space. A novel arrangement, at least as far as seventeenth-century royal dwellings were concerned, and one designed to suggest the equal political—if not marital—status of husband and wife. Both apartments contained an unprecedented number of bedrooms and a confusing array of beds, making it difficult to know who was sleeping where, and with whom, until after the construction of the Porcelain Trianon, the Sun King's glittering blue and white tile pleasure palace.

The Queen's Bedchamber was completed during Louis XIV's second building campaign, a so-called "peacetime effort." The mood of the day was brightly nationalistic, favoring the use of indigenous materials—marble from Languedoc and the Pyrenees, tapestries from the Gobelins workshops—despite the fact that the interiors themselves were Italianate in design. The Bedchamber ceiling, for example, was divided into multiple compartments, and everything in the room was banded in marble, contributing to an oppressive and oddly trussed feeling in all the Queens who slept there. So what if two immense pairs of floor-to-ceiling glass doors provided a fine view of the Orangerie, where, in clement weather, the potted palm trees stood row upon row like feather dusters, and, just beyond them, one could see the glittering rectangle of the Pool of the Swiss Guards, and Satory's wooded hills? Hadn't the Pool of the Swiss Guards originally been called Stinking Lake?

Marie-Thérèse died in the Bedchamber, as did Marie Leczinska, Beloved's equally long suffering wife. He replaced some of the marble with wood, most notably on the floor, added bronze doors, and hired Boucher to paint the ceiling compartments with *grisaille* celebrations of the Queen's virtues, all of which—lucky for him —had their roots in a dull and basically tractable nature.

Marie Antoinette hated the Bedchamber. She did what she could to make it a more congenial place, putting up giant mirrors festooned with gilded bronze lilies, getting rid of all the tapestries commemorating the Sun King's military victories, and covering the walls instead in a lustrous white *gros de Tours* embroidered with bouquets of flowers and ribbons and peacock feathers. Wherever possible she added fringes, tassels, plumes, and braids, as well as cramming in chiming clocks and footstools, wing chairs and dainty cabinets, which were in turn filled with lacquerware, crystals, jasper, sard, and petrified wood.

But nothing helped. A box is a box, after all, no matter how many pretty things you put inside it.

Meanwhile, in her thing-filled Bedchamber, Antoinette dreamed.

She dreamed that while she slept her keys were taken from her pockets, permitting anyone to unlock her desk and read her letters, while at the same time making it impossible for her to lock them back up.

She dreamed that while she slept she was being watched.

Sometimes it was her mother's face bending over her, scowling, checking for signs of disobedience.

Sometimes it was Mercy's face, masking disgust. Sometimes a complete stranger's.

The dirt-smeared face of a Savoyard, for instance, who seemed to have climbed onto the chimneypiece. Grinning and shouting words of encouragement as, meanwhile, a very hot fire burned near at hand, nearer than it should be unless it had somehow escaped the fireplace. Go away! Go away! The glass doors were caulked shut and pasted over with paper, and on all sides thick tapestry screens were held in place with rope, just barely protecting her from a great press of people, watching and whispering on the other side. The smell of vinegar, lavender, hyssop. A hand inside her, a hand on her stomach, and, shamefully, her naked body exposed from the waist down.

Such pain. Open the doors! Please!

But this was no dream, and the next thing she knew there was the Princesse de Lamballe's hand right in front of her face, her awkward overlarge fingers with their embarrassingly chewed nails making the private signal they'd settled on for *girl*.

All those chairs and clocks and mirrors and crystals and chimes and hands and mouths and noses sucking up what little air there was—first came a muffled thump as the Princesse fainted, followed by a low moan as the Queen followed suit.

"Warm water!" shouted the terrified accoucheur, who thought she was dying. "She must be bled in the foot!" But the room was so packed with princes and counts and countesses and foreign dignitaries as well as everyone who'd wandered in from the courtyard, not to mention all the furniture and knickknacks, that there was no way to get a basin of water through to him, and so he was forced to lance her foot without it. One quick jab and a jet of blood came spurting forth; naturally this cured her at once.

It was December 20, eleven o'clock in the morning; Antoinette had been in labor for eight hours. Louis smashed through the caulk and paper and glass, letting in gusts of cold winter air and a few flakes of snow. "Poor little thing," Antoinette is reported to have said to her daughter, "though you were not wanted, you will be my very own the more for that. A son would have belonged to the state, but you will be my happiness, and soothe my sorrows." Meanwhile the accoucheur, who would have received a pension of forty thousand *livres* for delivering a boy, did his best to hide his disappointment, wrapping the infant in blankets and handing her over to the Princesse de Guéménée. Through the broken panes the Orangerie terrace was barely visible, empty of palms, its two little reflecting pools glazed over with ice, staring blindly up at the lightless gray sky. A salute of one and twenty guns was fired, the meager number echoing the accoucheur's disappointment.

Two years later it would be a salute of one and a hundred guns, and the festivities celebrating the long-awaited birth of an actual heir to the throne would go on for weeks. In Paris the tocsin would ring without cease for three days. Fireworks would explode over the Seine, the fountains pump wine, and enormous heaps of meat and mountains of bread appear for the taking. Little Louis Joseph, decked out in gold raiment, would prepare to receive adoration as if he were the Baby Jesus.

Two years later delegations of tradespeople would come, bearing gifts: the chimney sweeps a miniature chimney with a regally clad boy crawling out the top, the locksmiths an elaborate and mysterious lock designed to release, when the King finally figured out how to spring it, a tiny Dauphin of steel. The whole world would come to pay its respects, and the whole world would be welcome, with the possible exception of the gravediggers, who'd be sent packing after showing up with a Dauphin-sized coffin.

Granted, it wasn't as though the birth of Marie-Thérèse Charlotte went completely unmarked. Prayers of thanks were offered for the opening of the Queen's womb, and it seemed possible, if only for a moment, that the French people might be willing to let bygones be bygones.

But only for a moment. Once it sunk in that Antoinette wasn't going to die, once word got out that her belly had been restored to its former supple state and that she was eating cream of rice with biscuit and a little poached chicken, everybody suddenly remembered how much they didn't like her. The Austrian Bitch—a big disappointment. Couldn't even be counted on to get the baby's sex right . . .

Marie-Thérèse Charlotte. Popularly known as Madame Royale, and nicknamed Mousseline la Sérieuse by her doting parents. A pretty child, with her mother's clear fair skin and large blue eyes, the older she grew and the more male siblings she acquired, the more her habitual gravity turned to sullenness, the sort of dusty limp look a sun-loving plant, a daisy for instance, develops when stuck in a shady part of the garden.

She would outlive them all, La Sérieuse, ending her days deep in the woods in a dark stone house, with only mice and squirrels and owls and the occasional fox for company. A persistent sighing of wind in the trees, a constant rain of leaves and acorns. A leaky roof, a smoking fireplace. Once upon a time she was a princess and she was crying because she was teething, and she was holding onto her father's finger as she sat on his lap in a wing chair covered in white *gros de Tours*. She loved to hold onto that finger, so long and plump and warm, with a consoling knob of knuckle in the middle and a smooth gold ring at the base. Big white clouds sailing past the window, and her father giving off his usual smell of sweat and horse manure and wine. Her mother playing the harp. Pling pling pling. I had a little nut tree and nothing would it bear.

La Sérieuse died in 1851 at the age of seventy-two, the same year Louis Napoleon proclaimed himself emperor. The house fell into ruins and was sold as scrap. Eventually the road to Quimper was built over the place where it had stood.

Voices from Beyond

The English-style garden of Montreuil, the Prince and Princesse de Guéménée's small yet graciously appointed chateau. It is a brilliant afternoon in early autumn, 1782; the Princesse is seated on a stone banquette, surrounded by her dogs. She is wearing a simple white lawn dress in the Creole style currently favored by the Queen, and a wide-brimmed straw hat, its blue ribbons loose and dancing in the breeze. Her eyes are closed.

PRINCESSE: How out of sorts I feel today, my darlings! Not unlike a soup tureen in the hands of a clumsy servant, if you know what I mean. Come closer. Speak to me. Set my mind at ease.

COOKIE: Hark, hark, the dogs do bark . . .

POUNCE: The beggars are coming to town . . .

PRINCESSE: Please. You're just making things worse. *She rubs her temples and sighs.* I want good news. Tell me some good news. The war in America? My dear friend Antoinette? Her adorable children?

WINNIE: Your dear friend Antoinette has an income of between three and four million *livres* a year.

PEARL: She also has one hundred seventy new dresses since January. White spots on a lavender ground. Gosling green with white spots. Mottled lilac.

LULU: Spots are all the rage.

WINNIE: Not to mention she's more beautiful than ever. Everything that astonishes the soul leads to the sublime—Diderot said that.

PEARL: Infernal depths, darkened skies, deep seas, somber forests. The war in America is over, by the way.

PRINCESSE: Hush, hush. You've made your point.

POUNCE: A clear idea is another name for a little idea.

He bares his teeth and growls.

COOKIE: Pounce is a very clever boy, but dangerous.

LULU: He's a very bad boy.

A shower of yellow leaves blows in from stage left; Pearl paws at the Princesse's shoe, whining.

PRINCESSE: This wind! If it doesn't let up soon I'm going to have to go inside.

PEARL: But I thought you wanted to hear about the adorable children. Don't you want to hear about them?

PRINCESSE: Yes. That's right. I do.

COOKIE: The little girl is solid as a rock, but the Dauphin's a mess. His vertebrae are put together wrong.

PRINCESSE: I'm their governess. All I have to do is look at them to know that.

CLIO, *angry:* Then what more do you expect? You of all people should know that the future is off-limits, even to the dead.

COOKIE: You of all people.

More leaves blow in; the dogs become suddenly watchful, tense, their muzzles raised, their ears pricked. The wind lifts the Princesse's hat from her head and carries it, ribbons atwirl, toward the chateau.

PRINCESSE: Stop please!

COOKIE: But we can't. We can't.

FLOSS: You of all people should know that we can't stop anything.

PEARL: Where the sheep is tied, it must graze.

COOKIE: Famine and pestilence.

WINNIE: Fire and flood.

Suddenly everything is in motion, the agitated dogs, the blowing leaves, the Princesse's gauzy white skirts. A combined sound of barking and snarling and howling can be heard, as well as the leaves' dry rattle and the flapping of fabric. And then, just as suddenly, the wind dies down; everything becomes perfectly still. By the time the Prince enters, stage right, the Princesse is paging through her breviary, and the dogs are lying in various postures of repose throughout the leaf-strewn garden. The Prince de Guéménée is a heavyset middle-aged man with a wild look in his eye. He is wearing a dove gray frock coat and tan riding breeches; his thinning white hair is braided into a pigtail and tied with a black ribbon.

PRINCE: Where on earth have you been, my darling? I've been looking everywhere, calling and calling.

PRINCESSE, *setting her breviary aside:* Nowhere but here, my darling.

POUNCE: Nowhere but nowhere, don't you mean?

The Prince sinks heavily onto the banquette beside the Princesse and heaves a loud sigh.

PRINCE: Then you haven't heard.

PRINCESSE: Heard what?

PRINCE: That we are ruined.

PRINCESSE: Indeed. *She laughs nervously.* And shall we have nothing to eat but pig swill from now on?

PRINCE: Please, my darling. Try to be serious. Our debt is somewhere in excess of thirty-three million *livres.*

PRINCESSE: Ours and everyone else's.

PRINCE: You don't understand. Debt is like building a castle in the air, stone by stone by nonexistent stone. To be free of a tangle you must borrow, to borrow you must be at ease, to be at ease you must spend. And then one day a real crack appears, and the whole thing falls in a heap at your feet. *He puts his head in his hands.*

LULU: Like faith.

OPHELIA: A castle built to the glory of God will never fall.

PRINCESSE: But you can't live in it, can you? *Can* you?

PRINCE: My darling, please try to concentrate. I've had to declare bankruptcy.

OPHELIA: With faith, two fish can feed thousands.

POUNCE: Not if there's a cat around.

PRINCESSE: You aren't answering me.

LULU: Death to the cats!

$\cancel{}$And if I had it to do over? Would I choose to live my life differently?

What a question!

Change even the smallest detail, the eyelash that got in your eye that summer night when Count Axel Fersen—beloved Axel!—spirited you off with him to the North Quincunx, and the next thing you know you're an old woman raising pigs in the Perigord. An ugly old woman with multiple chins and liver spots and a head where a head's supposed to be, attached to a neck, that is, which is in turn attached to a body.

Joséphine, he called me. A pet name, though of course I remained Antoinette, just as the Quincunx used to be called the Great Labyrinth.

They amount to the same thing, choice and fate. No one made me be Queen, and yet. "You took the trouble to be born, nothing more," wrote Beaumarchais.

Say goodbye to the eyelash in your eye and you say goodbye to your eye, as well. Eyebrow, eyelid. Antoinette, goodbye, you say.

Nor would you necessarily end up old and ugly and a woman. You could be King of Sweden, for instance, a handsome young count tucked firmly under your wing. You could be a butcher, a cow. Even the handsome young count himself, tucked there firmly yet, I have no doubt whatsoever, platonically, despite the King's famous appetite for handsome young men.

In the beginning the bodies stand empty, like milk pails waiting to be filled. Then the spirit is apportioned, completely at random, and once it's been poured in, that's that. There's no room for leaks or spillage. You can catch the measles from your brother-in-law. You can eat roast beef. You can take a lover, give birth. But no matter how close the proximity, it's only your flesh that's changed, only your flesh that sprouts a rash or puts on weight or bursts into sweat. No matter how close the proximity, you'll never end up with a trace of cow-spirit.

No matter how old you live to be, that is what you are, through and through. Like a tree, when it's sawed in half, or a body that's been torn to pieces by a mob.

It was the summer of 1784. Everyone said I was at my most radiant. I had my two dear children and was once again pregnant, in the early stage that leaves you flushed and bright-eyed and nauseated. My husband was busy making preparations for a French expedition to the Pacific. We'd won the war in America. My mother was dead.

I was in love.

The gardens around the Petit Trianon had been lit with log fires and fairy lights. Anyone who wanted could walk there after supper, provided they could still walk after dining on forty-eight entremets and sixteen roasts, and provided they were wearing white.

The white was my rule. I wanted everything to be perfect. Perfectly beautiful, the sky as dark and endlessly translucent as the Hall of Mirrors at midnight, the moon a dazzling milk white globe, and the courtiers drifting along the pathways in their white clothing like moths.

Everything perfect except, no surprise, my husband, who'd come out wearing shoes that didn't match.

I was in agony, I admit. As if the shoes were a moral failing.

Louis was keyed up, and not just because he'd spent the whole afternoon studying maps of the Sandwich Islands, but also because he wanted to make a good impression on the aforementioned Swedish King, who was considered at the time to be our best bulwark against Russia, as well as Europe's leading enlightened despot. A great theater lover, Gustavus enjoyed traveling incognito. Though unlike my brother he was quite the fashion plate, having made his entrance at Versailles disguised as Turkish royalty.

Louis said I was to spare no expense in planning a party. My favorite directive, even though I knew I'd come in for the same dreary criticism soon enough. Of course I had my own reasons for wanting the event to be a success, an occasion that would not only reflect the grandeur of the French court, but would also provide a brilliant setting for me, Antoinette, the brightest jewel of all.

Poor girl, so full of expectations! She had no idea, no idea at all . . .

We were to have a new opera, performed on the stage of the Trianon theater. Called *The Sleeper Awakened*, it was based on a story from the *Arabian Nights* about an ordinary citizen named Hassan who becomes a caliph and then falls in love with a slave girl. I'd chosen it myself, as it required the endless costume changes Gustavus was said to adore.

Poor poor Antoinette, turning this way and that in her chair to survey the audience. Where *is* he? Poor sad Hassan, renouncing his throne for love.

You can generally count on a sodomite to appreciate the company of witty and fashionable women; Gustavus clearly found me irresistible, or at least until it was time for bed. "The Queen spoke to all the Swedish gentlemen and looked after them with the utmost attention," he later reported, though whether he was slyly hinting at my attention to one Swedish gentleman in particular, who's to say?

Gustavus was a tall man with an extremely high forehead and the stubbornly impassive look of a sheep, though whatever his face lacked in expression he made up for with his hands, which were, as he was well aware, his finest feature. He wrung them to indicate anguish, fluttered them to show amusement, waved them around in time to the music. When he clapped, he held his hands absolutely upright as if getting ready to pray, so you couldn't fail to notice how long and graceful his fingers were, how exquisitely manicured his nails.

I thought the opera would never end, likewise the supper after it. Endless supper! Two hundred mouths, all of them endlessly opening, closing, chewing, chattering; two hundred bodies digesting, sweating, expelling gas. From time to time I'd catch sight of Axel, but since we hadn't been seated in the same pavilion it was always at a distance, my view partly blocked by some count's fat flushed face, some marchioness's towering hairdo. Pure and remote, Axel, like the north itself; he looked thinner than when I'd last seen him, darker, more melancholic— but that had been three years ago before he left to fight in America. Of course I had no appetite, not for food.

At last the musicians assembled on the terrace and began playing dances, their gigantic shadows sawing away madly on the wall behind them. Demented black shadows, smooth golden stone. Lilies and jasmine, boxwood and candle wax. When released into the sweet night air, the pent-up stink of two hundred bodies added its own crucial note, one that was welcome, seductive, even. Gustavus took off in hot pursuit of a coquettish little equerry; I could hear the sound of oars dipping in and out of the water, an oddly dry sound, like silk stirred by wind.

Antoinette! Antoinette! There was a game of hide-and-seek in progress somewhere near the Temple of Love, Artois hoodwinked and spinning, arms outstretched. Antoinette, come play with us! The grass was sopping, moondrops adrift on the water. No sign of Count Fersen anywhere.

The first time I saw him he was only eighteen, exactly the same age as I. At one of my Monday-evening masked balls, back in the days when Beloved was still alive, Louis impotent, and I was still a foreigner, my true identity pitifully obvious to everyone in the French court, despite the mask. A foreign body, Antoinette, like a piece of shot in a wound, something that has to be removed before it kills you.

We danced, we talked. Axel told me he'd been to visit Voltaire—all the young men did when they made their tour, as if the philosopher were a monument similar to Chartres or Notre-Dame. Voltaire's dressing gown was faded and his wig shabby, but he had beautiful soulful eyes, Axel said, almost as beautiful and soulful as my own. Of course they were all he could see of me; he had no idea who I really was until I lifted the mask. Just for a second and then I was gone, leaving nothing behind except, I guess, an impression. Gold hair, white skin. "The prettiest and most amiable princess I know," as he told his sister.

Nor did *I* forget *him*, oh no, oh no. And sometimes found myself daydreaming about him, recalling his brooding look and agile body, his fine dark eyebrows and air of underlying sadness, as meanwhile I sat glued to that gold brocade loveseat in Adélaïde's apartments, embroidering my lumpish husband one pathetic vest after another and thinking, *This is where I'll be stuck all my life without company or friends.* Sifting through the ashes, weeping floods of tears.

Sorrow kills men, they say, gives life to women. A woman's heart is more alive than a man's, if less bold, and so with that heart of hers a woman can endure whatever comes her way.

But, for now, he had come back. Axel had come back and the night was sweet, the grass wet. Everything was joy, dancing and feasting. Hide-and-seek near the Temple of Love, blindman's buff on the terrace. Little roast pigs roamed crispy through the park, an orange in each mouth, a sprig of parsley in each ear, a knife and fork stuck upright in each back—my husband lay on the Temple steps, insensate from overeating. Antoinette! Antoinette! A chorus of voices, every one of them begging me to come play, every one of them not Axel's.

I couldn't rest until I found him. Or, better yet, till he found me, a white moth adrift on the night breezes.

I was headed more or less in the direction of the chateau, though why, I can't say, except possibly to trick fate into giving me what I wanted by appearing not to want it very much after all. I passed couples in rapt embrace, both vertical and horizontal. I passed men and women relieving themselves, some behind trees, others in the middle of the path. It was well after midnight, Cassiopeia descending, Antoinette ascending. The night was dazzlingly bright, the canal clear as air, weeds and stones gleaming at the bottom, a clump of waving cress, a sparkling pebble.

Drifting moth, drifting, drifting, almost as if my feet never touched the ground. Almost as if I had no feet, only wings, a quickly beating heart.

Who knows where I'd have come to light if it weren't for the lash in my eye? It was driving me mad; I thought I'd die if I couldn't get it out. I turned my back on Apollo's snorting golden horses, the moon casting my shadow before me on the Tapis Vert. I blinked. I pulled down my eyelid the way Papa had taught me. To either side, dense plantings of trees, their heads not yet thick with foliage, and up ahead the lit windows of the chateau, out of which everyone who wasn't at the Trianon, chiefly old people and sick people and servants, grudgingly monitored the night's festivities. Of course I was too far away for them to see me.

Too far away for them to see me blinking, tugging at my eyelid. Too far away to see the man dressed in white detach himself from the trees and approach, a finger to his lips.

I felt very alive. My eye was watering.

"Your Royal Highness," he said. His French was perfect, without a trace of a Swedish accent.

I asked him why he'd been avoiding me all evening, and he put on an expression of amazement. "*I* avoiding *you*?" he asked, then took me by the hand and led me into the trees to the left. His skin was smooth and dry and warm enough to suggest great stores of banked fire deep inside.

"Joséphine," he said, and I heard a catch in his voice, almost as if he were a young man again and his voice just starting to change. "I've said something to upset you."

"But I'm not crying," I told him, laughing. "There's something in my eye."

He drew a handkerchief from his breast pocket,

licked one corner into a tip, cupped my head in his hand, and leaned in close. "Shhh. Don't move," he ordered. His breath always—always!—sweet like a child's, since he drank very little and never smoked a pipe and had adamantine teeth. My husband's opposite in every way but one, assuming, that is, I wasn't blind to the signs of true love.

"Better?" he asked.

"Now I get to make a wish," I said.

First the trees clustered thick around us, their trunks still giving off the day's heat, while the air that stirred between them grew cooler, darker. There was no pattern to their arrangement, and wildflowers clustered between their roots, anemone and violets. Little wild animals as well, rabbits, squirrels.

Axel guided our way through the trees, moving lightly but purposefully, his arm around my waist. I had no idea where he was taking me, and it was such a relief for once not to know—not to anticipate, you might say, the wheeling in of the toilet table after the wheeling off of the bathtub—that I didn't ask.

"I've told my sister about you," he said, looking down at me, his eyes black and avid. World of wild things, foxes, human glances. "She says she hopes the two of you will be good friends, and bade me warn you not to take my moods too seriously."

"You must give her two kisses—*here* and *here*—sister to sister, and reassure her that aside from matters of state, I take nothing seriously."

"Antoinette—"

"Shhh!" I admonished. "I refuse to listen. It's Midsummer's Eve. If you so much as *think* a serious thought, I will vanish into thin air. I promise."

"But it's only because I care about you, you must believe me. Antoinette, dearest. The world is changing. Hear me out. The people of France hate you."

"Thank you very much."

"No, look at me! Joséphine! They want a Queen without flaw, but they also want no Queen at all. When you sit among them in a Paris theater, dressed as they are, they call you common, and when you leave them for Versailles, and put on your diamonds, they call you traitor."

Of course these may not have been our exact words, though they're close enough, at least in spirit.

Just as the planting of trees which Axel guided us through may not have been to the left of the Tapis Vert, but to the right, meaning that when I finally turned to him and said that all I really wanted was for him to help me find a way out, it may not have been in the North Quincunx, but the South, where we suddenly found ourselves.

Of course I'd been there many times before, only never from that direction, through the thick, patternless woods. Never on Midsummer's Eve, never with Count Axel Fersen.

It was as if, in the midst of life's bountiful yet confusing array of details—bark and leaves and rabbits and eyes; moon and stars, even, warnings, kisses—we had suddenly been vouchsafed a view of death.

I say death, though I ought not.

Ought instead to explain that where once there had been no plan or pattern, where once the space around us had been filled with trees like the Bull's Eye Chamber with aimlessly swarming courtiers, with trunks and limbs and twigs and leaves and *nature*, we now found ourselves in a place where the trees had arranged themselves according to the principle of the five-spot in a deck of cards, with a tree occupying each of the four corners of a square, a fifth the center, and the whole motif extending indefinitely outward.

The same earth beneath our feet, the same sky overhead, and yet we might have been in another world entirely.

Not one tree too many, not one out of place.

What is more beautiful than the well-known Quincunx, which, in whatever direction you view it, presents straight lines?

So said Quintilian, who also said that the perfection of art is to conceal art.

Nor does it matter, really, if Axel was my lover, in

the physical sense at least. That isn't what matters, I know that now. It matters to historians, most of them men. It matters to gossips, most of them women. The pleasure is in the speculation.

My sister Carlotta made me eat sweet woodruff; it was early summer. My mother rode past us on her horse and for the first time I noticed they both had the same enormous buttocks. The air was fresh and blue, the grass new and green. Hope means if there once was a lash in your eye it will never be anything but that, no matter how old you live to be. Carlotta and I pricked our thumbs on a pricker bush; we mixed our blood and swore our undying love. You can always come back to a place, even if it isn't there anymore. The Labyrinth became the Quincunx, the Quincunx became nothing. It's always just *you*, even when your lover calls you Joséphine.

Inside the Quincunx, Axel and I were more alone than two stones at the bottom of a pool. It was the summer solstice; the nights were getting shorter, the dreadful winter of 1784 fast approaching.

LABYRINTH

There were thirty-nine fountains tucked away within the Labyrinth, and the Labyrinth itself tucked into a shady corner of the palace grounds, west of the Orangerie, south of the Latona Gardens, and north of the aqueduct carrying water to the town of Versailles.

Each fountain was based on one of Aesop's fables, though interestingly never on those about lions. The Monkey King, the Parliament of Rats, the Rooster and the Diamond, the Hare and the Tortoise — there were almost two hundred animals in all, all of them exquisitely cast in lead and gilt-painted, their gold mouths wide open, spewing forth bright jets of water.

The Sun King had the Labyrinth built for his heir, the so-called Grand Dauphin, alone among his six legitimate children to survive the court doctor's passion for bloodletting. A sweet-natured person, and also quite handsome until he grew fat, the Grand Dauphin. In the end the court doctors got him as well, leaving him empty as a glove, after which the Grey Sisters prepared him for burial. Or maybe it was the chateau floor polishers, or the workmen who made the coffin. Accounts vary.

Though when you think about it, isn't this the lesson of a labyrinth? You walk in filled with eager anticipation of the marvels that await you, racing along the boxwood-lined paths as if actually guided by some intrinsic sense of destination, only to find yourself in a dark little cul-de-sac, face to face with a gilt-painted lead rat on the back of a gilt-painted lead frog.

Of course the Sun King's intentions for the Labyrinth seem to have been somewhat less metaphysical. Aesop's pragmatic, you might even say *cold*, view of human relations deeply appealed to him, and he hoped to impress them by whatever means possible on the Grand Dauphin's dreamy sensibility.

The Labyrinth could be entered by means of a special key, in the keeping of Bishop Bossuet, the sadistic tutor. *Come, come,* Bossuet would implore in a fed-up tone. *For the love of God, lift your feet.* As often happens, the boy's gentle spirit stimulated the tutor's desire to inflict pain; soon enough Bossuet had beaten any love of learning out of his charge, who grew into what we'd call a nonentity if it weren't for the fact that he was heir apparent to the French throne. The Grand Dauphin loved playing card games, hunting for wolves, ugly women, and collecting art, though not necessarily in that order. Frequently he could be seen drumming his fingers on the lid of his snuffbox. "Like a ball to be rolled hither and thither at the will of others," according to Saint-Simon, "drowning in fat and gloom."

Bossuet would unlock the gate at the main entrance, flanked on the left by a statue of the fabulist himself, on the right by a statue of Love. Bowing, ironic—*After you, Monseigneur.* The Labyrinth astir with bees, the almost ducklike voices of the actual (as opposed to lead) frogs living in the thirty-nine fountains, the shifting shadows of millions upon millions of leaves.

Straight ahead, then right, then right again, then left. The Duke and the Birds. The Eagle and the Fox. The Dragon, the Anvil, and the File.

A Dragon wanted to eat an anvil, wrote Aesop. And there the Dragon was, disgruntled and golden, coiled in his shadowy lair with water shooting from his mouth and nostrils. *A File said to him, "You'll break off your teeth before you even begin to bite into that, whereas I can chew my way through anything."*

Meanwhile Bossuet stood waiting in his long black robes at the intersection of two paths, arms crossed, tapping his elegantly shod toe. Sun glinting off the crucifix on his chest, off the mammoth dome of his forehead. That pious half smile!

And the moral of the tale? Louis, please! How many times do I have to tell you to leave your nose alone and pay attention!

It's a miracle, really, that any of the royal children went on to become King. But maybe there's no version of childhood that could adequately prepare you for that particular future.

Louis XIV (the Sun King) begat Louis (the Grand Dauphin), who died after begetting Louis (the Duc de Bourgogne), who died after begetting Louis (the Duc d'Anjou), who luckily survived long enough to become Louis XV (Beloved) upon the death of Louis XIV in 1715.

Left, and left again, around a hairpin turn. Left once more. Backtracking.

The Monkey and Her Babies. The Fox and the Crane.

A she-monkey gave birth to twins, one of which she lavished with affection, the other, neglected. But by a curious twist of fate she hugged the one she loved so tightly to her breast that she suffocated it.

Tapping that toe, smiling that smile. It's said that once Bossuet actually broke the Grand Dauphin's arm, though certainly not from any overwhelming rush of love. Revenge comes cheap, however. The pleasure, for instance, of picturing a gilt-painted Bossuet with water coming out his nose.

The moral, Louis? The moral?

And how fitting, really, that the South Quincunx should have been built on the site of the Labyrinth. For while it's true that Louis XVI ordered the fountains dismantled and the sculpture packed away, the box-wood hedges mowed down and the latticework gazebos chopped into kindling (Oh Versailles! Oh grief! Oh ravishing glades! The hatchet is at the ready and your hour is come!), it's also true that traces of the Sun King's original Labyrinth remain. A ghost Labyrinth (like Louis XIII's hunting lodge, or the Porcelain Trianon, or the Ambassador's Staircase, or all the trees that were felled in 1774, or that got blown down by the wind, including Antoinette's beloved tulip tree), its maddening nests within nests of paths reborn as secret passageways and corridors, little rooms and littler rooms, closets and stairways, like the little secret stair in the wall connecting the Dauphin's secret gaming room with his father's bedroom. Only to be used in an emergency, advised his father, delicate.

And then Louis XV begat Louis (Dauphin of France), who died after begetting Louis (the Duc de Berry), who went on to become Louis XVI, husband of Antoinette.

The path on each side twisting sharply to disappear behind a wall of vine-covered lattice.

To the right? Or to the left?

A rat struck up a friendship with a frog who played a mean trick on him. He tied the rat's foot to his own, and when they came to a pond, he dived in and swam happily around while the poor rat drowned. But then the rat's dead body floated to the surface, where it was spotted by a kite, who snatched it up in its claws and ate it. The frog tried to untie his foot but he couldn't, so the kite ate him, too.

THE RAT
AND THE FROG

*An evening in late summer, 1785. Palais Cardinal, the Paris
residence of Louis de Rohan, Cardinal of the Holy Church
and Grand Almoner of France, as well as Landgrave of Al-
sace, Provisor of the Sorbonne, Superior General of the Royal
Hospital of the Quinze-vingts, Commander of the Order of the
Holy Ghost, and first cousin to the Princesse de Guéménée.
Rohan is a tall man with a big flushed face and rosebud lips;
his heavy legs, of which he is unreasonably vain, are crossed
at the knee and clad in bright red stockings. When the curtain
lifts he can be seen in rapt conversation with the seer
Cagliostro, a dark-complected man in a blue silk coat and
plumed tricorn hat who claims to have helped build the pyra-
mids. The two men are seated in enormous wing chairs in
Rohan's candlelit Salon of Monkeys, its dancing monkey
wallpaper dimly visible in the background.*

ROHAN: Tell me again.

CAGLIOSTRO: If you insist. *He lifts his head to the ceiling.* It is only a matter of time. Only a matter of time before the truth emerges, radiant, like the stars and planets at the behest of Isis, Goddess of Light. Only a matter of time before the Adored One ceases to dissemble and shows her true colors. Before she ceases to cut you dead in the galleries of Versailles, speaking of you, on those rare occasions when she does, with base contempt, with disgust even, with—

ROHAN: No. Wait. Go back to the part about the planets. The true colors.

CAGLIOSTRO, *irritated:* When you interrupt like that I lose contact with the Seventh House.

ROHAN: The Adored One. The Queen. Antoinette. Go back to that.

CAGLIOSTRO: If only you hadn't interrupted. *He returns his gaze to the ceiling, clears his throat, waits.* I'm sorry, it's no use.

Rohan puts a hand in the pocket of his frock coat and jingles some coins, lightly at first, and then, when there's no immediate response, more loudly.

CAGLIOSTRO: Perhaps I was too hasty. *He shakes his head, again clears his throat.* Unhappy lover! Take heart! Glory will come to you from a correspondence.

He stands and exits, stage right, as the woman called La

Motte enters, stage left. The room is no longer candlelit but sunlit, the wallpaper monkeys plainly visible, swinging from palm tree to palm tree or hanging by their tails. Rohan remains seated in his wing chair; La Motte perches on a low stool at his feet. She is a small-boned woman with masculine features and masses of chestnut hair.

LA MOTTE, *swatting Rohan's outthrust hand:* Not so fast! How about some refreshment first? It was hot enough today to poach a trout, the carriage was packed to the gills, and all there was to breathe was the breath of a dozen crapulous Goths.

ROHAN: Spare me the details. *He rings for his manservant.*

LA MOTTE: Ah, I forgot. The curse of the oversensitive nature—it must be a great burden. *She sighs, reaching deep into her bodice and extracting a blue envelope bordered in gold which she regards with feigned surprise.* But what have we here?

ROHAN: What? What is it? Don't tease. Give it over. Besides, you know I'll make sure you get what you deserve.

LA MOTTE: That's what I'm afraid of. *She sniffs the envelope.* You'd think by now she'd be sick of the smell of heliotrope. You'd think she'd have moved on to something a little more subtle, a little less cloying— goodness knows I've dropped enough hints. Though

while we're on the subject of teasing, for some reason I was under the impression you liked being
teased.

Rohan rings again, without result.

MALE VOICE, *offstage, singing:* "I may not be handsome, yet I know how to play. When the night gets
dark as jet, every cat looks gray."

FEMALE VOICE, *offstage:* "How sweet the breeze will
seem this evening in the pine grove . . ."

ROHAN: Servants! You can't do a thing with them.
They've all fallen under the spell of Beaumarchais,
that smooth-tongued scoundrel.

LA MOTTE: It must be a great burden, servants.
She tears open the envelope and begins reading. "My
Darling Jeanne, sweetest of friends, best of
confidantes—" And blah blah blah on and on in that
vein. The poor dear can hardly get enough of me. Of
course that's not what . . . Let's see. "One in whom I
can put my trust—" No. Wait. Ah, here we go. "Of all
the mistakes I've made in my life, and I admit to
having made quite a few, I suspect my harsh treat-
ment of R. is perhaps the worst."

ROHAN: R.?

LA MOTTE: Ramses, King of Egypt. Who do you
think?

*Rohan grabs the letter and takes it into a corner, where
he stands reading it to himself, as meanwhile a sullen yet*

good-looking young man suddenly appears in the doorway, shirt untucked and powdered wig askew.

LA MOTTE: Your master's not exactly a quick study.

FEMALE VOICE, *offstage, singing:* "When a man cheats on his wife—"

MALE VOICE, *offstage:* No no no! Just try to remember it's not a dirge, *chérie.* Try it again, only lighter this time.

FEMALE VOICE, *offstage:* You try it. It's an impossible tune.

YOUNG MAN: Perhaps I could be of some service?

LA MOTTE: As a matter of fact, I'm dying of thirst.

ROHAN, *waving the letter:* An assignation! The Queen suggests an assignation!

LA MOTTE: Why am I not surprised?

ROHAN: The Grove of Venus. Wednesday next.

The young man winks, reaching lewdly into his trousers while pretending to tuck in his shirt.

They all exit, stage right.

A scrim descends, stage rear, concealing the dancing monkey wallpaper. Though it's been painted to look like a formal garden in the moonlight, the room is brightly lit; a rehearsal of the last act of Beaumarchais's Marriage of Figaro *is in progress. Enter Antoinette, in the part of Suzanne, masquerading as the Countess Almaviva in a long white cloak, together with Artois, dressed as Figaro.*

ANTOINETTE, *singing:* "When a man cheats on his

wife, the world says he's a champ, but let his wife do likewise, and the world calls her a tramp. Who can possibly explain why the world is so insane? Because the men make up the rules, the men make all the rules."

ARTOIS: Better. Much better. But you're going to have to sing louder if you want to reach the back row. And at some point you've got to remove that cloak so everyone can see who you really are.

ANTOINETTE: Suzanne, you mean? Or Marie Antoinette, Queen of France? *She lets the cloak fall to the floor, singing:* "But let his wife do likewise—"

ARTOIS: Your secret's safe with me, *chérie.*

ANTOINETTE: I have no secrets.

ARTOIS: Just as I said.

They exit, arm in arm, laughing, stage right.

The lights dim and darken. In place of the scrim, an actual grove of pine trees, their branches forming a vault through which patches of moonless, starless sky can be seen, within which night birds hover and roost. The musical sound of nearby fountains, a statue of Venus visible, stage rear, pouring water from a ewer. Enter Rohan, stage right, his body enveloped in a dark blue cloak, his face hidden by a broad-brimmed hat; when he reaches the center of the grove he is approached by a woman wearing a white lawn dress identical to the one worn by Antoinette in Élisabeth Vigée-Lebrun's most recent portrait and holding a single long-stemmed red rose. Though the woman has the Queen's ash blond hair, blue eyes, and remarkably good figure, she is in fact a Palais Royal streetwalker who goes by the name of Oliva.

ROHAN, *kneeling to kiss the hem of her skirt:* Dearest!

OLIVA, *handing him the rose:* You know what this means.

She races off into the shadows, stage right, and the curtain falls.

NECKLACE

It was hideous, an abomination. It looked like a collar a circus horse would wear, a huge clanking thing in four tiers (not counting the knotted tassels and pendants), consisting of 647 diamonds the size of robins' eggs. It weighed more than the Dauphin. The Queen wouldn't have been caught dead in it.

Created for Madame Du Barry by the court jewelers, Böhmer and Bassenge, the necklace in question was of a type called *rivière*, as in river of diamonds, and was the discerning benefactor's gift of choice for his Palais Royal whore. "*Rivières* flow very low," sneered the pamphleteers, "because they're returning to their source."

Unfortunately Louis XV died before he had a chance to pay for the necklace, and despite Böhmer's best efforts to interest Marie Antoinette—even threatening to hurl himself in the Seine if she refused to buy it—for a while it looked as if the jewelers were going to be stuck with the thing. The diamonds in it were worth over one and a half million *livres,* not to mention the time that had gone into its creation. Böhmer and Bassenge were desolate, desperate. They were two nice Belgian men, getting on in years, alone in the world, without a leg to stand on.

And then, melodrama!

And then, a miracle!

Jeanne de La Motte, who was a very shrewd woman, managed to convince Cardinal Rohan, who was a very silly man, that the Queen secretly loved him, even though everyone knew she'd despised him for years. La Motte conjured a heady mix of romance and the occult, of love letters and a starlit assignation—finally tricking the Cardinal into authorizing the purchase of the necklace on behalf of his Queen.

Once the jewelers had handed the necklace over to La Motte's lover, disguised as the Queen's private courier, he immediately broke it into pieces and began to fence it around Paris and London. "I love imagining the most beautiful diamonds in the world on the world's most beautiful neck," Böhmer said in a note to Antoinette, which she burned to bits, going on the not unreasonable assumption that the man was mad.

That neck! Rohan was baffled. That perfect white neck, but why was it not wearing the necklace? Candlemas had come and gone, and still no sign of it. The skin so smooth, so white, so creamy and delicious! That perfect white column where he longed to press his lips.

He couldn't believe it when the King had him arrested on the Feast of Corpus Christi, and sent him to the Bastille. His lawyer spread the news that he was languishing there in irons, but in fact he was lounging in a very comfortable apartment, dining on oysters and drinking the finest wine.

Popular sentiment held that Rohan exhibited an "excess of candor," meaning everyone knew that he was stupid. Meaning everyone knew he was somehow worthy of their forgiveness, of their love. He was tried before the Parliament of Paris and acquitted on May 31, 1786.

The necklace ceased to exist except as a diamond here, a diamond there. A pair of pendant earrings. A brooch. A single stone hidden in a black velvet bag in a mahogany box, traded for a snuffbox and a pair of silver asparagus tongs.

ROHAN'S ARIA
(after Beaumarchais)

ROHAN (*singing*)
>Slander's like a gentle wind,
>a gentle zephyr pitched so low
>you hardly feel it, till it lightly,
>oh so sweetly starts to grow.
>Piano, piano, slowly seeping,
>sotto voce, softly creeping,
>slyly sneaking, deftly slipping,
>faintly humming, lightly tripping,
>as the storm begins to blow.
>First a mere insinuation,
>then a hinted accusation,
>what began as innuendo
>all at once starts to crescendo,
>louder, bolder, brazen-sounding,

stomping, beating, thumping, pounding,
screaming, banging, booming, clanging,
spreading horror through the air . . .

November. My thirty-third birthday. Day of the Dead, 1788. Beasts howling in the forests. Ice like diamonds. Every night at dinner the water froze in the jugs. Every night at dinner the King gorged himself on roast meat and wine. His eyes got smaller and yellower, he quoted Milton. The Dauphin was getting weaker; the Dauphin was dying. He didn't want to eat. The idea of eating three meals a day bored into his brain like a worm into an apple.

> *Fly envious Time, till thou run out thy race,*
> *Call on the lazy leaden-stepping hours . . .*

Was ever a woman so sad, ever a woman so hopeless?

Yes, Antoinette. Probably all of them, if truth be told. Brave women, stuffing rags in their shoes, foraging for bread in the streets of Paris. Brave murderous women, if truth be told, since what woman would hesitate for a second if she thought that by murdering someone she could save her own precious child's life? People in Paris were black with hunger, Axel said. Each night forty newborns were left on the doorstep of the Foundling Hospital. People were making straw effigies, Louis the Crack-Brained, Madame Deficit, and setting them on fire to warm their hands and feet. The Seine was frozen solid as a rock. Frozen water everywhere like a message from the future.

> *Then long Eternity shall greet our bliss*
> *With an individual kiss;*
> *And Joy shall overtake us as a flood.*

He had quite a memory, my Louis.

The Diamond Necklace Affair was finally over, Rohan back in his palace, writing his memoir; Cagliostro duly idolized, writing a memoir. The little streetwalker Oliva's memoir had already been published and branded a great popular success. The only one of the key players left in prison was La Motte, and when she escaped everyone said it was through my influence. We'd been lovers, it was said; she was my cat's-paw. The whole thing had been her idea, so you'd expect her to have had a good imagination (or at least as good as every other French citizen busy picturing his Queen lavishing attention on one cock after another; so many cocks, said the author of "The Patriotic Bordello," that if they were laid end to end they'd stretch from Versailles to Paris), but she didn't. La Motte ended up all by herself in a filthy room in London, writing memoir after memoir. Eventually she threw herself from a window.

Maybe it's that whatever passes for imagination in a conniving mind has very little to do with hope. Hope is the ability to imagine other ways out, at least when you're young. Later it changes into something else.

The passageway from the South Quincunx, for instance, via the vanished Labyrinth. Imagine that passageway, like something a small animal might tunnel, twisting and turning around tree roots and past glittering fountains, through the Land of Dancing Water, the Land of the Singing Apple, the Land of the Little Bird Who Knows All, and to Eternity. The long Eternity that would greet our bliss.

Back then I was thirty-three going on a hundred. My hair was turning white.

Nor was I thinking of anything so fanciful as Eternity. No, what I was really thinking of were Axel's apartments, that labyrinth of rooms I'd had built for him just above my own, tucked into long forgotten hallways and within walls, between second-story ceilings and third-story floors, folded in so perfectly you needed to count footsteps or use a tape measure to know they were there, a maze of secret corridors and cubbyholes accessible through doors you could only barely make out, the faintest seam in a panel of silk wallpaper, in a gilt molding, the whole thing a little on the dark side but giving onto a small courtyard and with enough mirrors so that you could count on the occasional ray of morning sun to kiss your skin.

From the South Quincunx, through the Labyrinth, and into Axel's arms.

"Close your eyes," I told him. I led him into the room where the new Swedish stove stood ticking in the corner as its dark blue tiles heated up. Tall, from floor to ceiling—it had been next to impossible to sneak it in without anyone noticing, but I'd managed. Maybe the more obsessed the people around you are with rumors, the less observant they are of what's actually going on. Maybe the busier they are reading "A List of All the Persons with Whom the Queen Has Had Debauched Relations," or discussing how the Queen paved the floor of the Trianon with jewels, or pondering how the Queen got the King drunk on purpose in order to have sex with—of all people!—Cardinal Rohan, the less they see.

Axel said it was a beautiful stove, he couldn't have been happier with it, and I started to cry.

The logs were green and wet, the chateau reeking of smoke. All the windows were thick with frost; you couldn't see through them, let alone open them, even a crack.

He was so kind. It was more than I could bear. Not just the pamphlets, though they were bad enough. Not just my sweet sickly boy. My baby girl, born in July, dead the following June, her lungs the size of teaspoons. The Serious One, my own dear daughter. She heard I'd fallen from my horse and said she wished I'd died.

"Dear heart," Axel said. "Joséphine." He'd chosen that name because he said it made him think not only of the softness and paleness of my skin and hair, but also the firmness of my chin, which he loved. I couldn't stand having anyone around when I was miserable; he took my chin in his hand, he looked me in the eye. "She didn't mean it," he said. "She's very harsh; that's her way. It's how she protects herself. She'll live to be a hundred."

From the north, Axel—the frozen north. If you were to split the frozen surface of the Grand Canal with an axe, out would flow blood, warm red blood. He didn't mind if you saw that about him.

Wicked men, monsters! What had I done that they should hate me so?

A proper Queen would stay in her apartment doing needlework, everyone said. A proper Queen would never have gotten mixed up in the Diamond Necklace Affair in the first place.

No smoke without fire, everyone said, except Goethe, who said the affair filled him with as much terror as the head of Medusa; or Napoleon, who referred to it years later as the gateway to my tomb.

Generally speaking, men are more melodramatic than women.

Meanwhile the Dauphin was dying. He was getting thinner by the day, his poor little spine more and more twisted and his poor little face pinched with pain, every single breath costing him the greatest effort. Lying flat on his stomach on the green felt billiard table in the Chamber of the Pendulum Clock, reading history, philosophy. Reading Hume's *History of England*, like his father. Our expectation that the sun will rise tomorrow has no basis in reason, but is a matter of belief, which is why it should have come as no surprise to Charles I to wake up one fine day to find his head chopped off.

The two beautiful clocks tick tick ticking away.

Even the surviving Mesdames, Adélaïde and Victoire (Sophie died in 1782) couldn't remember a worse winter. Paris was in chaos; things weren't much better at Versailles. We handed out food to the poor; we built bonfires at the crossroads near the Grand Canal. Food and bonfires, just as Louis's cousin Philippe, the Duc d'Orléans, was doing in Paris, though unlike him we didn't try suggesting that no one else was doing anything to help.

But Philippe was busy becoming ringleader of the

opposition, turning the Palais Royal, his Paris residence, into its headquarters. The Duc d'Orléans—a true Prince of the Blood but otherwise Colonel in Chief of the Emptyheads, a man best known for enjoying rabbit hunting in the nude. "I'm stunned by the pleasure of doing good!" he exclaimed, though that was merely that devil Laclos, who also happened to be his private secretary, speaking through him.

Did I say frozen solid? Did I say reeking of smoke? Did I say four walls do not a prison make?

With a polite nod of the head this footman or that would indicate that hidden door or this; we still thought things weren't so bad. We still thought we had choices. I'll tell you a secret. We ran out of wax candles and had to use tallow; the whole palace smelled like sheep.

You can either refuse to give up hope or you can sink into the deepest of depressions. Eventually the horrible winter will turn to spring, no matter what. Your beautiful clocks will keep marking the hours, days, weeks, months, movements of the stars. Also, your bosom will get bigger, forty-four inches. Your husband will develop eczema. He will become increasingly despondent, unable to decide anything.

"It is the doom of our great ruling line to rest inert at some poor halfway house," said the Austrian playwright Grillparzer, "deaf to the call for strenuous endeavor."

Which is why even though I knew that Charles I's fatal mistake was to listen to his wife, I also knew it was time to interfere.

Eventually the horrible winter was over. Everyone was in a better mood because Louis had taken my advice and brought Necker back as Minister of Finance. Liverish, self-satisfied Jacques Necker, with his prissy pursed lips and his understated cravats and his sanctimonious wife, Suzanne. "Savior of France he shall be," everyone was singing, *"Alléluia!"* As if he could actually turn back the clock. Late spring, the days mild and sweet. White asparagus, red *fraises des bois.* Lent had come and gone, making *"alléluia"* once again permissible.

The dying Dauphin sat propped on cushions by his window, eating the jujube lozenges I'd sneak to him against the doctors' orders and watching the twelve hundred deputies to the Estates-General march in procession across the three toes of the goosefoot, from one side of town to the other. Blue sky and white clouds, a fresh spring breeze. The parish priests wore black wool robes, the noblemen black silk outer coats, the Third Estate plain black suits and black tricorn hats. I had a circlet of diamonds around my head, a little heron feather in my hair.

Twelve hundred deputies. Twelve hundred and one, if you counted both faces of the Duc d'Orléans. Robespierre, Mirabeau, Talleyrand. Of course you had no way of knowing who would emerge as a hero or a villain before it was over.

Of course, then, you had no way of knowing there was going to be an "it."

After the sun had gone down the air grew chill; the Swedish stove kept burning all night long. Through the open windows came the sound of inflamed oratory, songs, cheering. Kill the rich! Liberty! Democracy! Axel described the swamps of the New World to me, tree trunks like elephant legs caparisoned in lacy green moss. In America they were wearing steel buttons and steel shoe buckles, a Republican fad that was just beginning to catch on here at Versailles, along with no wigs, no panniers, no jewels, and clothes the color of goose droppings. In Paris you could see me and Louis and the Dauphin sitting under a baldaquin at the Wax Museum, dining with Voltaire, Rousseau, and Benjamin Franklin.

Axel, my knight-errant from the north. Axel, with his brown eyes and heart of fire. He wasn't especially witty, unlike everyone else at Versailles; it was a great relief, really. When urged to plight his troth with Necker's ugly daughter Germaine (the future Madame de Staël), he said it was impossible. He'd never marry, he said, since the one he loved was already taken. I always wore dark colors in his rooms, deep red, deep green.

Were we sexually intimate? What difference could it possibly make to you?

I wrote a song for him: He is my friend, give him back to me. I have his love, he has my trust; I have his love, he has my trust.

The Estates-General continued to meet. The Third Estate convinced most of the clergy and noblemen to put aside their separate identities and join in a National Assembly that would draft a Constitution and keep meeting even if the King ordered it not to, which, as it turned out, he didn't, but instead issued a proclamation ordering all the deputies to join the National Assembly.

Happy days in Versailles! Music! Fireworks! We made an appearance on the balcony, the whole royal family, and only the wife and mother was seen to look a bit the worse for wear, letting her white hair hang loose to her shoulders, like a citizeness.

Whereas in Paris the bread was getting worse and worse. It was made from bad-smelling yellowish flour and had lumps in it you needed an axe to cut, and when you ate it it tore your throat and made your stomach twist with pain. Even so, people fought for the scraps like dogs. In Paris the doors of the nobility were marked with a big black *P*, meaning "proscribed" or condemned to death, though, really, it was the nobles and not the peasants who were the spearhead of the Revolution.

If the canaille can't have any bread, let them eat straw.
That was Laclos.

Mirabeau, a confirmed Orléanist, said that to depend on the Duc d'Orléans was like building on mud.
Chateaubriand said that I had a beautiful smile. Talleyrand said that no one knew what pleasure meant who
hadn't lived before 1789.

To arms!!! yelled Camille Desmoulins. People were
setting the customs barriers on fire, breaking into the
gunsmiths' shops, looting the stores of grain. They broke
into the cellars of the Hôtel des Invalides and stole
twenty-eight hundred muskets and ten cannon.

That was in Paris.

On July 14, when the citizens of Paris were storming
the Bastille, Louis once again wrote *Rien* in his journal,
just as he had on our wedding night so many years earlier.

Everyone was leaving Versailles. Sneaking out side
doors and windows, dressed as nobodies.

Goodbye, Rose Bertin! Goodbye, Polignacs!

The night the Dauphin died, the four tallow candles
on my dressing table went out one after another, all on
their own. A flaw in the wicks, said Madame Campan, the
eternal optimist.

Even under the best of conditions, the trip from
Paris to Versailles took three hours.

GOOSEFOOT

Eleven miles from Paris to Versailles, from the Chaillot tollgate to the Place d'Armes. Rain's been falling steadily since morning, small fierce winds tearing through the woods that line the highway, scattering brown and yellow leaves in the mud. Four miles from the tollgate to the river, then another seven to the gates of the palace. A long slow climb up a long easy valley. October 5, 1789.

Everyone knows the danger is in Paris. In Paris everyone's hungry and the bloodlust is universal except, interestingly, among butchers. The summer's harvest was good, so why is there no grain? Because the Queen is hoarding it, say the pamphlets; because she wants revenge for the way she got treated during the Diamond Necklace Affair. The Queen is a glutton. The Queen wants to make her subjects starve, especially the women, to pay them back for judging her so harshly. As if she doesn't deserve it—a discredit to her sex!

The women of Paris are gathering at the Hôtel de Ville, that gargantuan eyesore. Fishwives and market women and women from the floating laundries on the Seine, as well as a number of men dressed up like women. Meanwhile, Laclos's agents are running around handing out money and brandy. A man of diverse talents, Laclos, with his long tapering fingers and his tragicomic genius, his endless fascination with desire's many deadly faces, not to mention his skill as a pamphleteer. The Queen is a dog in the manger, for instance. A dog in the manger sitting there in her big fancy palace like a brood hen on a mountain of bread, though generally he doesn't mix metaphors like that. Some of the women brandish kitchen knives or skewers; some of them beat little drums. Some of them are singing: *If the rich love gold so much, let it melt in their yaps. Voilà the sincere wish of the sluts who sell fish.*

It's raining in Paris, it's raining in Versailles.

"It's Raining, Little Shepherdess," sings the Queen's musical clock. If only she were a shepherdess. They should have moved court weeks ago, left for Metz, Compiègne, Soissons. But would the King budge? Mr. All Frenchmen Are My Children?

Three roads lead into Versailles and three lead out of it: to Saint-Cloud, to Sceaux, to Paris. Le Nôtre's famous goosefoot, like the footprint of a giant mythic creature. An immense bird that landed once, balanced there skeptically on one leg to regard the marshy landscape, and then took off. The palace gates haven't been shut in over two hundred years; the palace gates are rusted open, in fact.

Such a gray dismal day, so windy and wet. Of course the King and Queen aren't afraid of a little water.

He's gone hunting in the ancient forests of Meudon, she's headed off to her fairy-tale village just beyond the Petit Trianon. She's wearing a plain linen dress and a plain lace cap because that's what she likes to have on when she milks her two dear cows, Brunette and Blanchette. She'll milk them, and afterward she'll take a pail of milk still warm from their udders and sit on a mossy stone bench beside the millpond while she drinks it from a ladle. Yellow leaves drifting across the pond's gray rain-pocked surface, doves cooing in their cotes. The table silver's been sent to the mint, also the silver toothpick cases and the silver bucket she washes her feet in, all to help relieve the bread shortage. "I am the father of a big family entrusted to my care," confided the King when she complained. Yellow leaves, poplar leaves, orange Chinese goldfish. The smell of wet moss. White geraniums and a few roses still in bloom, though the wind and rain are sure to finish them off before the day's out.

Eleven miles from Paris to Versailles.

From Chaillot Gate to the banks of the Seine, the river foam-flecked and moving fast. A long slow climb up a wet gray valley. Seven miles to go. The women are shouting, *Bread! Bread! Bread!* The highway's like mush, their shoes filled with mud. *Hang the Queen and tear out her guts! Rip open her belly and jam in your arm! Cut out her liver! Give me a thigh! I'll have a breast! I've got her heart!*

They hold up their sodden mud-splattered aprons, pretending they already carry pieces of the Queen. They sharpen their knives on the milestones. They lick their lips.

What does it mean when thousands of women march through the mire, their shoes getting ruined, their brains changed to blood? Does it matter that they were lied to? That Versailles is beautiful, a dream of Paradise, their Queen bewitching, the trees turning gold?

Something that's held for hundreds of years is blowing apart.

"I've never been afraid in my life," says the King to the servant who's been sent to fetch him home from the forest. A bad day's hunt, interrupted (as he'll later write in his diary) by "events." He's drenched, not unlike the Queen, who hardly has time to finish her milk before she, too, is fetched back. Wrapping her cloak around her heavy wet shoulders, though her gait's every bit as springy and girlish as usual—she never looks back, not even for a moment.

By late afternoon the Place d'Armes is black with angry Parisians. Roaring and screaming, waving knives and skewers and brooms, they press their mud-soaked bodies against the gold rails of the fence separating them from the three inner courtyards, where a double rank of the Royal Bodyguard just barely manages to hold them off. *Cut the Queen to ribbons! Make cockades of her guts!* They spill away from the fence, darkening the three toes of the goosefoot. They jeer and howl. They pull their skirts over their heads.

Versare, to return—the presumed Latin root of *Versailles*. As in, turn the soil and then, having done so, turn it again, over and over, until it's perfect. Which it never will be.

At some point you leave a place and that's that. At some point you reach the point of no return. Though often enough you don't know you've reached it. Don't know this is your last chance to drink in the least tiny detail, the way your entire room is contained in miniature in the crystal globes hanging at the bottom of each of your chandeliers, for instance. Miniature bed, miniature harp. Rain dripping from the eaves, shining on the stones of the Marble Court.

"I refuse to run away," says the King, claiming he'll

calm the unruly spirits with kindness, which he actually does, for a while at least. He promises grain, he agrees to meet with a delegation of women, one of whom—a pretty young girl named Pierrette Chabry—is so overcome with emotion at being in his presence that she falls to the floor in a faint, after which the King himself administers smelling salts and lifts her to her feet.

In any case, things are looking up. The National Guard has finally arrived, led by Lafayette on his snow white charger. The Queen can't stand him, never could, calls him a "simpleton Caesar" even though he's devoted to her. But then the Queen hates to feel beholden to anyone.

Besides, she *wants* to run away. To the beech forests of Compiègne, the bridges and canals of Metz. Or even farther, to the Land of the Midnight Sun, where no one bats an eye if they come upon a polar bear walking down the street.

Rain pounding on the windows, rattling down the gutters. By now most of the Parisians have found shelter at Versailles, either in the King's stables or under the canopies of the portes cocheres or in a tavern or a church. Some of them are sleeping, some are wide awake and getting drunk and making plans. A horse is being roasted on a spit over a roaring fire in the middle of the Place d'Armes, and some of them are eating it. Two in the morning, wind blowing from the southwest. Each thinks himself a Brutus and sees a Caesar in each noble. All of them are wet as ducks.

Quiet now, but soon enough an angry group will break into the Cour des Princes and swarm through the palace, smashing down doors with axes, looking for the Queen. Through the Salons of Hercules, Abundance, Diana, Mercury, and Apollo, down the long Hall of Mirrors and through the Salon of Peace, past the snoring body of Lafayette—henceforth to be known as General Morpheus—collapsed on a couch, and into the Queen's apartments. Soon enough they'll hack off the heads of two of her guardsmen and stick them on pikes, before stabbing through the Queen's bedclothes and into her mattress, stabbing again and again and again, though she won't be there, having fled earlier to the Bull's Eye Chamber, where she'll be cowering, stockingless and in her petticoats, waiting for dawn with her sleepy optimistic husband and her two darling children and her lumpish brother-in-law Provence and his mean-spirited wife and her two ancient aunts-in-law Adélaïde and Victoire and the brand-new governess and all the ministers and servants who won't have gotten away yet and, yes, even her lover. Even Axel Fersen.

It's too late; there's nothing anyone can do. They're going to get hauled back to Paris.

Yet why should it be sad, the end of privilege?

Why should it be sad that Marie Antoinette never sees the Trianon again, except for the fact that it's always sad when anything ends forever.

Sad to think that a beloved place should forever be denied us, water dripping into a millpond, a cow's soft brown nostrils. The smell of grass on her breath, of rain on moss. Her moist brown eyes.

Laclos, for instance—what made him tell the women of Paris that their Queen was sitting on a mountain of bread, unless he wanted them to be "in the picture," spoiling it?

Where would you hide a leaf? In a forest.

Where would you hide a pebble? On a beach.

Where would you hide a Queen? In a palace.

Where would you hide a peasant? In a mob.

As if it were a mystery, and there were a way to solve it. As if it were possible to figure out who slipped up, and where.

The Baker and His Wife

October 21, 1789. A bakehouse in Paris, near the Halle aux Bleds, its door chalked with an X. It's early morning, the sun just appearing over the lopsided chimney pots of the Marais; a beautiful bright autumn day is dawning. Gradually a small crowd assembles in front of the bakehouse door.

CROWD:

The hunger-swollen belly, restore, restore.
The hunger faintness, restore, restore.
The hunger drooping, restore, restore.
The utter famine, restore, restore.

They begin pounding on the door, politely at first, and then with increasing fury.

After several moments the door opens and the baker's wife peers out. She's a middle-aged woman of medium build, whose clothes and hair and face and arms are so completely covered in flour it's impossible to tell what she really looks like.

BAKER'S WIFE: Can I help you?

SKINNY YOUNG MAN, *mimicking her:* Can I help you? What kind of question is that?

BAKER'S WIFE: You'll have to excuse me, sir. We've been up all night baking.

BAKER, *offstage:* Tell them to come back in an hour. Tell them there'll be bread enough for everyone in an hour.

BAKER'S WIFE: An hour. You heard him.

SKINNY YOUNG MAN: I can hardly wait.

The baker's wife closes the door; immediately the crowd once again begins to pound on it.

PRETTY YOUNG WOMAN: Those eyes, that lip. Am I crazy, or does she remind anyone else of a certain royal someone . . . ?

CROWD: Open up! Open up!

SKINNY YOUNG MAN: Yes! Open up now or I'll huff and I'll puff and I'll blow your house down!

FAT MAN: They think they can hide from us. They think they're so smart. *He picks up a stone and throws it at the window.*

GRAY-HAIRED WOMAN: Who do they think they are?

The door is flung open, this time by the baker himself. He's a middle-aged man, tall and heavyset, his flour-dusted features even more difficult to make out than his wife's.

BAKER: Didn't you hear? An hour. First the wheat was late to the mill, and then there was no salt.

SKINNY YOUNG MAN: Of course. And the moon is made of cheese. We know you've got bread in there.

The fat man grabs the baker around the neck and hauls him out the door.

FAT MAN, *menacingly, in the baker's ear:* Do you love me?

CROWD: Feed my sheep.

FAT MAN: Do you love me?

CROWD: Feed my sheep.

FAT MAN: Do you love me?

SKINNY YOUNG MAN: They say the third time's the charm. *He yanks the baker's head back by the hair, then shoves him to his knees.*

CROWD: Feed my sheep.

The crowd quickly closes in, making it difficult to see what happens next. There's a raised arm, a scream, a flash of light as the sun glints off the blade of a large kitchen knife. A pool of blood begins to spread at their feet, spreading wider and wider; the gray-haired woman turns to address the audience.

GRAY-HAIRED WOMAN: The roots of the wheat plant are thin and form letters, as anyone can see who digs them carefully enough. The letters run on and on in the dirt before breaking and crumbling

away; you can never get them all out. But you *have* to
get them all, you have to find all their branchings for
the letters to spell a word, the word of happiness.

PRETTY YOUNG WOMAN: Who's going to find that
word now, the way the world is going?

CROWD:

Round the earth oven, restore, restore.

Round the hearthstones, restore, restore.

Round the foundation beams, restore, restore.

Round where the road starts.

*The skinny young man suddenly raises a pike on which
he's impaled the baker's head high above the crowd. Blood
continues to pour in a steady stream from the baker's severed
neck; the crowd breaks into loud cheers.*

BAKER'S WIFE, *peering through the broken window*:
Oh my God! Oh no! My darling! *She puts her face in
her hands and sobs.* He was only trying to do his job.

SKINNY YOUNG MAN, *lowering the pike and position-
ing it so the baker and his wife are face to face, mocking*:
My darling! My darling!

BAKER'S WIFE, *angry*: He was only trying to give you
what you wanted.

FAT MAN: He should have thought of that when he
told us to come back in an hour.

PRETTY YOUNG WOMAN: He should have thought of
that when he was born.

Holy Week, and fingers tapping lightly at my window. Mama? Come in, come in, but it was only the rain, pattering on the new leaves of the chestnut trees and lilacs, soaking into the lawn. Filling the hole my little boy dug just that afternoon with his toy spade, attended by six bored grenadiers of the National Guard. A cool afternoon, storm clouds assembling in the west. Storm clouds darkening the far-off sky above Versailles, turning the surface of the Grand Canal to melted lead, and sending all the birds our way.

They love to dig, boys. Left to their own devices they'll dig forever and their cheeks will grow pink with exertion, their eyes like the eyes of the blind, fixed on invisible objects. Until they hit an impossibly big rock, that is, or their governess sails forth to fetch them home.

We'd been in the Tuileries for almost half a year. A monument to squalor and decay, the Tuileries. A prison disguised as a palace. Every mattress damp and swarming with silverfish, though at least by spring we had actual mattresses to sleep on instead of piles of clothes and billiard tables.

"Kings ought to proceed in their career undisturbed by the cries of the people, as the Moon pursues her course unimpeded by the howling of dogs," wrote Catherine the Great in a letter. "When Kings become prisoners," I wrote her back, "they haven't long to live." I had to write all my letters in cipher, and hide them in a chocolate box.

Spring rain, Tuesday of Holy Week. My leg hurt. My left leg, which I had injured at Christmas, our first in the Tuileries. "How will Père Noël know where to find us?" my little boy asked, and, really, I had no good answer. My darling Dauphin, my *chou d'amour.* "Let's hope he doesn't," replied his sister. "He's probably a Jacobin, in that red hat of his." I'd been racing to close the curtains, to block the faces mouthing threats at the window, when I felt my ankle twist.

Now my whole leg throbbed under the weight of the rest of me, which felt dead by comparison with the throbbing leg, and that leg, in turn, grotesquely heavy. Once I'd been light as a feather. And where was the girl with the cherry red lips? Still there, I suppose. Preparing to enter history, like her mother before her.

On the windowpanes? Just water.

On the skin? Just nothing.

No hand stroking back the hair.

But when I dragged myself from my solitary bed and down the long long hallway of the Tuileries—limping past the scaffolding and the pails of gilt and plaster, the smoke-darkened billiard room where Provence was lining up yet one more corner shot and Louis, having polished off yet one more roasted haunch of some poor dead creature, was noisily licking his fingers—and at last came limping into my daughter's room, overwhelmed by the wish to stroke her smooth blond hair back from her smooth white forehead, she swatted my hand away.

Such a cruel system, mothers and daughters. From the fear of being humiliated, deliver me, O Lord. Of course the God who made our world chose to put suffering and death at the heart of it. We are weak, like the Disciples, and our love is always disappointing.

For the past year she had been studying the catechism, the Serious One; the next day, Spy Wednesday, she would make her first Communion.

From the fear of being lonely, deliver me, O Lord.

From the fear of being forgotten, O Lord, deliver me.

Even then my daughter knew that tenderness had never saved anyone's life.

Outside the window the sound of pipes and drums; the sound of spring rain and with it the smell of gunpowder. That was the mood outside the Tuileries, while inside we strove to keep up appearances. The eternal *lever*. The eternal *coucher*. The eternal cavagnole. Dance, nobleman, dance, I could hear someone singing. Dance, meaning *hang him from the lamppost*.

I looked down at my sleeping daughter and imagined her kneeling before the Bishop in her white gown and shoes, her hair safely tucked beneath her white veil. An earnest expression on her face, as usual—her father's own daughter. The altar rail sweet with beeswax, the whisper of pages being turned, the delicate bones of her hands tightly clasped in prayer.

I could imagine that. I could imagine no further.

GRANDES EAUX

From the Seine, from the Eure, from the Bièvre, from the Yvette, a vast underground network of pipes, some made of pottery, some of lead, some made of wood or cast iron, mile upon mile of them tunneling through the rich black dirt of the Île-de-France before suddenly breaking free as aqueducts, their troughs filled with sparkling river water destined for Versailles. The rivers keep flowing no matter what the people living around them are up to. They keep filling the arched vaults of d'Orbay's immense reservoirs even after they're no longer needed, the people who relied on them for baths or fountain displays having run away the previous fall, taking refuge here and there throughout the countryside like mice.

It was Louis XIV who set the whole system in motion, sick as he was of the disgusting quality of the water he inherited from his predecessor, so green, so thick, so bad-smelling. "Never," wrote Madame de Sévigné in a letter to her daughter, "have I heard anything more agreeable than what you told me about this great beauty soon to appear at Versailles, fresh, pure, and unaffected, who will put all others to shame."

Later she'd be surprised to find out it wasn't a young woman her daughter had referred to but a river diverted from its course by an army of forty thousand men. So long as the Sun King strode the face of the earth, his dark curls gleaming with health, his virility bursting from every pore, it was possible to believe that, when summoned to him, even the water would arrive girlishly submissive and eager to jump into his bed.

Now it's June. The Swan drifts across the surface of the night sky, trailed by the Shepherd's Star. Time to pick the new greens, garden cress and chervil, lamb's lettuce, rocket, and sorrel. Also time to replant. Leeks, scallions. Turnips, cabbages, endive.

Meanwhile the rivers continue filling all the reservoirs of Versailles: d'Orbay's immense churchlike cisterns under the Water Terrace, three shallow rectangular basins along the Rue des Reservoirs, a water tower slyly hiding behind a *trompe l'oeil* facade on the Rue du Peintre-Le-Brun, a deep cylindrical holding tank on Montbauron Hill. The rivers fill the reservoirs and then spill from them into Versailles's many pools and lakes and canals. The Mirror Pool, the Pool of the Swiss Guards, the Nymphs' Bath, and the Grand Canal, as well as the basins of all the fountains, Latona and Saturn, Apollo, Flora, Bacchus, and Neptune. The fountains themselves aren't running, since no one's there to turn them on. Even if someone were, it would be a terrible waste—the usual display requiring over 220 gallons of water per second!—since also no one's there to watch.

The rivers feed the reservoirs that feed the millpond in the Queen's little village. Last fall's yellow leaves never got scooped away and now they're black and scummy, adhering to the banks or floating on the glaucous surface of the pond. The silver milk ladle is lying near the stone bench right where the Queen dropped it, its handle snapped in two. The orange Chinese goldfish are dead.

Before he made his getaway last October, Monsieur de La Tour du Pin saw to it that all the buildings were boarded up tight, with massive iron locks clamped on the gates, and guards standing sentry. A place under siege, Versailles, yet even so the sky is clear and blue, not a single cloud in sight. An abandoned place, sorrowful, yet things are coming back. Mignonette and starflower, anemone and rue. The water lilies are in bloom, the doves cooing and guarding their nests in the roof thatch. The farmer and his wife are still living in their little cottage on the far side of the wheat field, tending all the animals the Queen left behind—including the babies she'll never get a chance to feed, all those lambs and bunnies and chicks—and milking Blanchette and Brunette twice a day, though no longer into porcelain basins, but into tin pails.

MIRABEAU

Early morning, July 3, 1790. A carriage has drawn up to the
back gate of the royal estate at Saint-Cloud, where the King
and Queen have been allowed to spend their summer months,
provided they return to Paris every week for Sunday dinner.
As the curtain rises a cloaked figure emerges from the car-
riage: Gabriel-Honoré Riqueti, the Comte de Mirabeau, a
tall man with a body like a wrung sock and a big head
sprouting dark bolts of hair he wears stuffed into a taffeta
bag. Mirabeau has described himself as "the mad dog from
whose bites despotism and privilege will die," but he's also a
man who enjoys the finer things in life, specifically wine,
women, and song, and happens to be, at the moment, heavily
in debt. Today he has an appointment with the Queen, with
whom he hopes to strike a deal: if she will agree to settle with
his creditors and give him a sizable pension, he will give her
and the King the full benefit of his persuasive powers in the
Assembly, where he is currently leader of the dominant party,
the Patriots.

As the coachman wanders off, stage right, yawning and stretching, Mirabeau leans into the carriage and addresses his nephew, barely visible at the window.

MIRABEAU: If I'm not back in half an hour, contact the Militia. *He disappears through the gate.*

We can see the nephew's bored face. It is, after all, quite early, the sun is warm, the birds are singing. The light is the kind of morning light that looks so fresh it makes you thirsty. Blue-gray shadows of linden trees flicker across a length of the chateau's honey-colored wall. The nephew falls asleep and begins to snore.

Enter two servants, stage left, an old man and an old woman, both wearing white aprons. The woman is carrying a bucket.

OLD WOMAN: Could you hear what they were saying?

OLD MAN: Eh?

OLD WOMAN: Oh, for heaven's sake. You and I both know there's nothing wrong with your ears.

They lean against the back of the carriage. The woman sets down the bucket; the man slips a loaf of bread from under his apron and begins to eat.

OLD WOMAN: The way I'm thinking, *she's* the one who wants to go, *he's* the one who wants to stay.

The old man keeps chewing. The sun brightens; the sound of birdsong gets louder.

OLD WOMAN: They tell me she hardly touches her food. Sends her plate back untouched. *She stares pointedly at the bread.* They tell me her hair's coming out in handfuls.

The old man pretends to cry.

OLD WOMAN: That's easy for you to say.

OLD MAN: I didn't say a thing.

They continue leaning against the back of the carriage, the man chewing, the woman watching him.

OLD WOMAN: Are you planning to eat all of that?

The old man smiles, nods.

OLD WOMAN: You're not even going to give your dear friend Héloïse one little bite?

OLD MAN: I might, if she weren't so disagreeable.

There is the sound of a door slamming closed, footsteps on gravel.

OLD WOMAN: Try to look busy. *She removes a wet rag from the bucket and begins washing a fence post.*

OLD MAN: As long as I live, I'll never get used to you.

Mirabeau approaches the carriage and raps on the door; his nephew wakes with a start.

NEPHEW: Back already?

MIRABEAU: She asked me to kiss her hand. *He is clearly overcome, emotions playing across his big face, its surface as pale and crater-pocked as the surface of the moon.*

NEPHEW: And did you?

MIRABEAU: Of course. *He pauses, looking back at*

the chateau. You should have seen her. I've always thought her admirers must be exaggerating, but now I know that everything they say is true. Even after all she has suffered—when she led me into the garden, I swear her feet never touched the ground. She is an angel. An angel with brains. The King has only one man near him, and that is his wife. *He opens the carriage door and begins to climb in, then stops to cast one final glance at the chateau.* Of course I kissed her hand. She is very great, she is very noble, she is very unfortunate, but I am going to save her.

Mirabeau settles himself in the carriage; the coachman takes his seat and shakes the reins. Birdsong and sun, linden light and shadow. A beautiful summer morning.

OLD MAN: The boy's right to ask. You don't want to kiss something if you don't know where it's been.

OLD WOMAN, *singing*: Oh, it'll happen, all right. It'll happen. We'll have no more Kings, we'll have no more Queens . . .

I thought I was going home. *Home*, that is, and not Versailles. I could hear the sound of children at play, little children speaking German, *guck mal! guck mal!*, and the wild splashing of a marble fountain in bright northern sun, instead of rain, more rain and thick gray skies and black umbrellas everywhere you looked. We used to slide in our stocking feet across the sun-bright floors of the Great Gallery at Schönbrunn, Max and Carlotta and Antonia and poor dead Joseph. *Starrkopf*, Mama called him, the Stubborn One. Just as she called our father Mousie.

"Take two days every year to prepare for death," he suggested in his little notebook. "Have no particular affection for any one thing and, above all, have no passion."

For your life, I guess he meant.

The hands of the beloved on your shoulders, their

heat and weight and pressure. The beloved's hands, binding you to the earth. As if there might be something wrong with desiring the alternative.

Slip away. Shh.

And in the end the signs of your passage erased little by little, fingerprints on cutlery, sweat on bed linens. Traces of your body, that sweet, faltering companion, as opposed to the more durable evidence of a signature, a treaty, an embroidered vest, a lock.

I prepared for death every day. I kept a bottle of oil of sweet almonds with me at all times, to use as an antidote, since I was evidently surrounded by people who wanted nothing more than to poison my morning roll or the sugar I liked to stir into my water at bedtime.

Of course I had trouble sleeping. It was never quiet in the Tuileries, though the noises weren't festive as they were at Versailles, but mostly furtive, a muffled dragging and bumping all night long. On the other side of the window the streets of Paris, generally wet and spreading out forever around us, Rue de Rivoli, Rue de Castiglione, their curbs like rivers and the river itself swollen and brown and heedless, longing to leap its banks.

Sometimes the weather cleared, but then there was the terrible prospect of the stars, a whole black sky full of them, exploding and falling . . .

Bitch. She-wolf. Pig.

Names *can* hurt you.

Those men in the Assembly, who did they think they were? Marat, with his bad skin and his bad temper. Prissy little Robespierre, with his carrying little voice.

As for Mirabeau, he'd proved to be no help at all, despite the money I continually forked over. Fan the fires of disorder until a longing for the old order returns —that seemed to be the extent of his so-called advice, after which he proceeded to spend a passionate night with a pair of opera singers, and died. Poor Mirabeau! Two years of rest before the Jacobins dug him up and carted him off with the carrion to the knacker's yard.

It was a mistake I made more than once, thinking a man could help me, thinking he was powerful enough to do me some good just because he was a man. I didn't want to be the powerful one.

I didn't want to be like my mother, though after a while I think I began to understand the way she'd seen her life, all the people around her so inert, so stupid. Like the beautiful gauze-winged dragonfly imprisoned in amber, a gift from King Gustavus. A treasure, Louis said, and he used it as a paperweight.

Home. I wanted to go home, or at least as far as Metz.

Besides, everyone was leaving Paris. *Everyone.* I ordered a traveling armoire, a huge thing with drawers and compartments, and packed it full of dishes and knives and forks and dice and decks of cards and chamber pots. Mirrors. Candlesticks. A manicure set. During the last year we had all changed size and shape, Louis growing fatter and fatter, myself thinner and thinner, the Serious One growing breasts and hips, and the Love Cabbage, just turned six, never managing to remain the same size or shape from one minute to the next.

Have I mentioned that his hair was the color of caramel? That it was thick and curly? That his legs were plump and strong? That I loved him more than life itself?

So hot, the summer of 1791. Hot and humid and wet, steam rising from the camellias in the Tuileries Gardens, from the flower beds, the paving stones. Mercy had been called back to Vienna; Necker had resigned. The clergy had been ordered to ignore the Pope and swear allegiance to the State. My brother Leopold, like most of the other European monarchs, was busy saving his own skin. We were being spied on through keyholes. "Go fuck yourself," said my usually mild gentle husband, when Lafayette proposed the first of several escape plans.

From Meaux to Châlons to Pont-Sommevel. Sainte-Ménéhould, Clermont, Varennes. Dun, Mouzay, Stenay, Baâlon.

Away from the blurred rain-drenched sound of

Meaux to the snow-covered peaks of the mountains.

Away from *here* and to *there.*

To Antonia standing on that island in the middle of the Rhine over twenty years ago, completely naked, her Austrian gown pooling at her feet. The pavilion walls flapping in a sweet spring breeze. Birds chirping, goose bumps on her skin. Bare knees and bare elbows. Navel. Little naked girl—and if she knew then what I know now?

Never go back. YOU WILL NEVER GO BACK.

You will leave everything behind. Everything. Every buckle, every clasp, every pin, every ring.

On June 20 we put on disguises and sneaked from the Tuileries; I was a governess dressed in brown.

In a specially outfitted berlin we flew through the night, out the city gate at La Villette and generally eastward, the Marne unspooling to our right like a length of moonstruck silk. A clear night, very hot; the children fell asleep almost immediately. "By the time we get to Châlons," Louis confided, "I will be a completely different person." We ate cold meat and rolls, I even drank a little wine. The sky began to grow lighter, roosters to crow in all the farmyards; eventually we could see fields of wheat, fruit trees and houses.

I remember feeling happy, looking out the window at the new day. Almost as if I were doing exactly what I wanted for the first time since I'd been forced to leave Vienna when I was fourteen years old. I saw a round blue pond with white ducks swimming on it. A dark-faced woman wearing a green-and-black-striped shawl. I saw a field red with poppies, a field yellow with rape.

We veered north into the long shadows of the Argonne Forest; it seemed cooler, though it was still hot.

Then the berlin had an accident, going over a bridge. Then the soldiers didn't wait for us in Pont-Sommevel, or anywhere else along the route for that matter. Then we got caught.

I thought it was like an ant trying to climb out of a teacup. All those painstaking small steps up a steep smooth wall, across tiny hand-painted forget-me-nots and rosebuds and the next thing you know you're back where you started. Back in the Tuileries, back in the mess at the bottom of the cup, and the people of Paris are out of their minds with joy. They're organizing street fairs, sending up hot-air balloons. They're hanging thousands and thousands of lanterns in the Tuileries Gardens, as if the idea of hanging lanterns from trees was something they'd only just come up with, and not something I'd been doing at Versailles for years.

PEAR TREE

Delicate, girlish, all in white. Like a girl dressed for her first Communion but with hints of the bride she'll one day be — among the five hundred pear trees in the King's Fruit and Kitchen Garden, Bon Chrétien d'Hiver's fruit is the sweetest, its habit the most graceful.

Jean de La Quintinie planted the first pear trees at Versailles in 1679, on a square plot of land just to the east of the Pool of the Swiss Guards. He divided the square into sixteen compartments of equal size, using the trees as walls, and added manure, peat, sawdust, and compost, since the soil was swampy and unwholesome.

"It is above all necessary that a kitchen garden please the eye," he wrote, "the most beautiful form being one in which the corners are carefully squared . . ."

He was a genius, La Quintinie; he could grow anything. He could give the Sun King asparagus in December, lettuce in January, cauliflower in March, strawberries in April.

He was also an artist, understanding as an artist must the difficulty posed by edges, transitions.

So Élisabeth Vigée-Lebrun handled the problem in her final portrait of Antoinette, the skin of her friend's face and neck and shoulders and arms an opaque smear of titanium white over dark translucent glazes, an almost mercifully obscure picture of where a body stops and a world begins, of how a Queen conceals her sadness.

So the roots of the pear trees extend beneath their shadows and deep into the dirt, while the white crowns dance indistinguishable from the cloudy sky.

That first summer, the summer of 1790, the first summer after the fishwives escorted the King and Queen to Paris, the pear trees set fruit and there was no one there to eat it. The fruit should have been picked before it was fully ripe, sometime in early September, and left to ripen in a cool room. It shouldn't have been left to ripen on the trees, falling to the ground where it got bruised and rotten, attracting wasps. The fruit should have been brought to the Queen on a Sèvres platter. She should have quartered it with a silver fruit knife, removing the core and delicately peeling away the skin.

"Bon Chrétien d'Hiver is of a yellow color," wrote La Quintinie, "and with a pink blush on the side which gets the sun, rejoicing the eyes of those who come to look at it as they might a jewel or a treasure. As for taste, it is incomparable, with brittle slightly scented flesh and sugary juice."

The trees bloomed in the spring of 1790, and again in the summer of 1791. No one pruned them or dressed them with manure. The white flowers opened, five-petaled and in clusters of six or seven. The petals fell off and the pistils began to swell. Some of the trees were attacked by midges, others by borers. Wasps buzzed hungrily around their feet.

The asparagus kept coming back, also the strawberries, though the beds were getting choked with weeds. Vagrants traveling from Saint-Cloud along the southernmost toe of the goosefoot would stop at the Kitchen Garden and fill their stomachs and their pockets.

There is no such thing as a bad-tempered pear, said Jean de La Quintinie.

When he died in 1688 the Sun King was inconsolable. Eventually the pears made their way to America, where they were called Bartletts.

Spring, summer, fall, winter, spring, summer, fall. Pentecost, haymaking, Saint John's Eve, Michaelmas, deer hunting, winemaking, Advent. You think it will go on that way forever; the days get long, the days get shorter. The pigs have babies, the pigs get slaughtered. Acorns. Willow wands. Lard.

At Versailles there were so many mirrors! I had most of them put there myself, and when I caught a glimpse of the Queen walking by in all her majesty it would please me, even surprise me a little, to see those blue eyes I'd been looking at my whole life still looking back at me, like a friend. Mama's silver hand mirror in Schönbrunn Palace, the reflecting pool beside her summer house. Your eyes will stick like that, Antonia, if you're not careful.

Not so many mirrors at the Tuileries, though—*grâce à Dieu, grâce à Dieu*.

Not so many mirrors here and no one playing the harp in a far-off room, a long thread of music winding back through the hallways to tangle round your heart. *It's raining little shepherdess. Ach du lieber Augustin.* The music box Carlotta gave me when she was dying and Papa took away because he said it made me morbid. *Alles ist weg, weg, weg...*

Princess Snowflake, Princess Bright-Eyes. What do you do, take them out at night and polish them?

"Our family life is a kind of hell," I wrote Axel. Everyone had taken to calling Louis "King Log," most notably Provence and Artois, as well as the rest of our fair-weather friends who'd eventually decamped for Koblenz, and as if to prove them right he'd stopped talking or doing much of anything except for playing backgammon with the Serious One, who was looking more like him with every passing day.

Though did it matter, really? At her age I was already married, a Dauphine. At her age I thought my whole life lay before me.

Sometimes we were allowed to go to the Princesse de Lamballe's salon, once to the theater to see *Psyche*. The Furies shook their torches as they danced, lighting our faces.

Sometimes I barely recognized myself and had to pause to realize that this person was really me.

"Tranquillity hangs by a thread," I wrote Axel, trying to get his attention. I sent him a gold ring inscribed *Lâche qui les abandonne,* after wearing it myself for two days to take the chill off. Coward, to abandon me!

Ach du lieber Augustin, all is lost, all is lost . . .

And then, one day I looked up. Late winter, lambs being born, also kids and fuzzy yellow ducklings, but it made no difference, I scarcely went anywhere.

I was looking up more those days, holding my head up high, as they say—it gave me a certain perspective, ceilings, birds, clouds, rooftops. Chandeliers. Hot-air balloons. The indifferent sun and indifferent moon as opposed to the expressions on the faces of the people around me, my dejected family, my pitying servants, the occasional furious Jacobin holding a calf's head aloft on a pike at the window, sticking out its tongue at me while its eye sockets buzzed with flies.

Holding my head up high and more than usually aware of my throat, where I used to paint a thin blue vein on top of the thick white makeup we all had to wear in the good old days at Versailles. Full of arsenic, that makeup— though when has it ever been safe to be beautiful? When has it ever been safe to be Queen?

The Blade of Eternity was busy flashing away out there in the weak Parisian sunshine. Monsieur Guillotin's brand-new idea, designed to sever the heads from the bodies of rich and poor alike in less time than it took to blink, or so Madame Campan informed me, having made a point of watching the trial demonstration on a petty criminal, a man convicted of forgery, in the Place de Grève. Nor did the forger's headless body commence to dance, as scientists predicted it might, nor did his bodiless head jabber in the basket.

Though who knows what ghostly thoughts kept flying through the hallways of the forger's brain?

A particularly challenging signature? The extreme forward slant of the capital *A*? The ornate flourish trailing from the final letter?

Or maybe his mistress's mouth preparing to smile, her upper lip lifting to reveal the white tips of her teeth and on her breath the smell of the season's first apricots?

Maybe *So this is what becomes of Eros.*

Maybe OH NO OH NO OH NO OH NO.

One evening in February, I looked up and saw a tall man with a large dog walking into my room.

He was wearing a disguise but I recognized him immediately, just as he did me. Even without mirrors I knew I was no longer slim and pretty, or not so slim though still pretty and vivacious, or verging on fat though radiant; even without mirrors I knew I was pale and haggard and white-haired.

But you can't have let your defenses so thoroughly down with someone and not forever after know them, no matter if they're disguised as a common messenger, like Axel that February day, flying on his winged feet past twelve hundred murderous guardsmen. I saw the melting snowflakes in his black eyelashes. I saw the set of the mouth, a dimple to either side of the faintly trembling lips, the brow no longer smooth yet still wide and intelligent, the nostrils flaring a little with each breath.

The dog was as long-legged as its master, a snow-white creature with pricked ears and a beautiful plumed tail that made me think of the ostrich feathers on my bedposts at Versailles. As I stood there rigid with longing, it leapt up and licked my cheek.

"Odin," Axel said. "Mind your manners."

And then he embraced me and, really, I thought a person could lose her head forever and what difference would it make.

Only later — much much later, the next day in fact — when Louis finally joined us, did the talk turn to politics. We were flirting with danger, Axel said. Flirting, he repeated and threw me a look; we were playing both ends against the middle, wooing every crowned head in Europe on the one hand, every bloodthirsty revolutionary on the other. It was too late, Axel said; our only hope was escape. Just because the last attempt had failed was no reason not to try again. We could head northeast this time, concealed within the dark tunnel of forests that stretched from Paris to the marches of Flanders. Why not? he pleaded, but of course we all knew perfectly well that even if escape had once been possible it no longer was. Not only was every avenue fiercely watched, but Louis had pledged his word to the National Assembly that he would stay in Paris, and Louis was an honorable man.

"If you stay you will die," Axel said.

"When the counterrevolutionaries finally get here," Louis replied, "the revolutionaries will need to keep me alive as a hostage to save themselves."

The human heart is many-chambered; I loved them both. I loved the touch of both men, the one seeking to calm my blood, the other to heat it up. The one froglike in his unfashionable wig, the red sash of the Order of Saint-Louis straining across the immense hill of his belly. The other tall and thin. On edge, watchful. Like a racehorse. A beacon.

Resté là, Axel would later write in his diary. This was his usual method for recording an amorous liaison, the equivalent of Louis's *got one*, but without the bloodshed.

MARBLE COURT

Quick, quick, along the Avenue de Sceaux. Quickly. Quicker. Sky the palest blue, every trace of color wrung from it by the heat, and off to the left on the far side of the stables and the tennis court, the Sun King's Kitchen Garden, its trees still standing in orderly rows, their boughs heavy with fruit. Pears, apples, apricots, plums. A drift of leaves underfoot, though it's too early, really, the second week in August, the wind from the east and hot.

An unendurably hot wind, breath of the Devil, ovens of hell. Eleven miles to the east, Paris is on fire. The Tuileries have been set ablaze, the royal family herded off to be locked in a tiny cage behind the rostrum of the Legislative Assembly, where everyone can keep an eye on them. "What a lot of leaves!" the King was heard to observe as he and the Queen were making their way along the crowd-filled Terrace of the Feuillants, her face red and blotchy, her bodice stained with sweat.

The wind raises dust from the cobbles of the Parade Grounds, dust and heat phantoms, transparent carriages, shimmering men and women, laughing, rippling, breaking apart.

Let us go, children of France, our day of glory has arrived . . .

Glory, yes! Let us go!

Four hundred steps from the first of two ornate golden grilles to the second, their gates padlocked, their gilt paint chipping off. Sun directly overhead and out of the wind now. Trash and leaves, dust and grit. Seventy-six steps across the Royal Court and then *tap tap tap tap tap* up five long stairs and you're almost there.

Almost.

Sun beating down. Down the row of wheat I've run and now my story's almost done . . .

Eleven miles to the east, the young Napoleon Bonaparte watches the goings-on at the Tuileries from the second-story window of a nearby furniture shop. The Knights of the Dagger, all of them old and infirm, together with a mixed bag of cooks and grooms and laundrywomen and spies and members of the Swiss Guard, are being thrown from the flame-filled palace windows, sometimes their entire bodies, sometimes just their heads.

Day of glory! Let us go! Little children catch the heads

and impale them on sticks. The greenery runs red with blood.

Even after Russia, Napoleon will say he never saw such carnage.

And what of the fat pig that has cost so much to fatten? Let him drink! Let him get drunk! Since Nature has given him a porker's character, let him live on as a porker!

And his tigress wife, meowing sweetly, biding her time till she can scratch again?

Lock them in the Temple, throw away the key!

Leaves and phantoms, Prudence and Mars.

Sun beating down and the way so long. Sun so hot and your heart so broken.

Fifty-seven steps to cross the Marble Court, from the top of the five stairs to the front entrance. All the doors and windows boarded up and the clock stopped at half past ten. Black paving stones, black ones and white ones, 11,520 marble paving stones in all.

Diligence and Peace, Wealth and Hercules.

Eleven miles to the east, the Tuileries turns to ash.

Eleven miles, no more, no less.

Let me in! Let me in! Let me in!

GEOGRAPHY LESSON

The Temple, an oppressive medieval fortress in the Marais. It is a rainy autumn night, the month of Brumaire, Year One of the new Republican calendar. As the curtain rises we see Louis Capet and his wife, formerly known as the King and Queen of France, seated with their two children at a candlelit wooden table, the Jacobins having papered the walls behind them to resemble the inside of a prison. Louis is in the process of making a puzzle map for his son, who is doing his best to stop coughing long enough to finish his bowl of soup. Antoinette is embroidering pink roses on a white seat cover; the Serious One is scowling into space.

LOUIS: Could you hand me the scissors, dearest?

ANTOINETTE: Just a moment. *She surveys her work critically, tries to snip the thread, and throws the scissors on the floor.* I give up! I hate these things! You couldn't cut butter with them, let alone someone's throat.

LOUIS: Dearest . . . *He reaches across the table to touch her hand.*

ANTOINETTE: I'm sorry. Ignore me. It's just that I'm freezing to death. You'd think they could at least keep the fires going.

SERIOUS ONE: When you get upset like that you get spots all over your face.

ANTOINETTE: Thank you.

She sighs and returns to her sewing; Louis retrieves the scissors from the floor and, with an expression of deep concentration, begins cutting a large piece of paper into smaller pieces.

For a while there is only the sound of snipping and coughing, and then other sounds, muffled at first but growing louder and louder, rattling chains, plodding footsteps, sliding bolts, keys turning in locks; the candles gutter as a heavy oak door bangs open, stage left. Enter the Tisons, the elderly couple hired to "look after" the royal family, each wearing a long white apron and a red Jacobin hat. As Citizeness Tison removes the Dauphin's soup bowl, Citizen Tison stands directly in front of Antoinette, blowing smoke in her face.

Antoinette stares fixedly at her work and keeps on sewing.

LOUIS: Excuse me. I don't think the boy was finished yet.

CITIZENESS TISON: He doesn't think the boy was

finished. *She spits in the bowl and hands it back to the Dauphin.* A thousand pardons.

LOUIS: Please. He's just a little boy. He hasn't been well.

DAUPHIN: It's all right, Papa. *He covers his mouth to stifle a cough.* I had plenty, really I did.

CITIZENESS TISON: Papa—that's a good one. *She elbows her husband.*

CITIZEN TISON: Will there be anything else?

He and his wife make their exit without waiting for an answer, slamming the door behind them. Once again there is the sound of turning keys, sliding bolts, rattling chains, plodding footsteps, fainter and fainter.

The Dauphin breaks into uncontrollable coughing; Louis puts his head in his hands.

ANTOINETTE: I can't take it anymore.

SERIOUS ONE: It's not like we have a choice.

LOUIS: Shhh. Shhh. *He rouses himself and hands the Dauphin a blank map of Europe, with a pile of cut-out countries.* We must at least try to be kind to one another.

SERIOUS ONE: But I'm only telling the truth.

LOUIS: Shhh.

He kisses the top of his daughter's head. The candles flicker; the Dauphin, still coughing, removes the top cut-out from the pile and squints at it.

ANTOINETTE: You have it upside down, darling. Here, let me . . .

DAUPHIN: I know that. *He turns the cut-out around.* I knew that all along. It's England.

LOUIS: The Kingdom of Great Britain . . .

DAUPHIN: That's right. *He sets it in place.* And this one's France. The *King*dom of France. And this is Prussia. And here comes *(walking his fingers across the map)* the Duke of Brunswick. Leading the armies of the Holy Roman Empire! Coming to save us!

ANTOINETTE: Oh yes. The Duke of Brunswick. Except don't you have him going in the wrong direction? Shouldn't he be headed *away* from France? And, come to think of it, shouldn't that be the Republic of France? And shouldn't he be running?

Louis rises stiffly from his chair and makes his way around the table to stand behind Antoinette, gently rubbing her neck and shoulders.

ANTOINETTE: The Duke of Brunswick. The Duke of Brunswick is lower than mud.

LOUIS: It isn't as if he didn't try to help us.

DAUPHIN: The Duke of Brunswick is lower than slime!

LOUIS: Of course I suppose we'll never really know the whole story of what happened at Valmy.

ANTOINETTE: Trying to help us! Everyone knows he

threw the battle. He was our last best hope and he sold us out.

LOUIS: We don't know that. His men were sick; they didn't have enough to eat. The weather was bad.

ANTOINETTE: I do.

DAUPHIN: The Duke of Brunswick is lower than shit!

SERIOUS ONE: Make him stop, Papa. He's driving me crazy.

LOUIS, *smiling:* I'd like to see the person who could do that, sweetheart.

And then. And then they took him away.

And then they cut off his head.

When I tried to sleep, my ear on the pillow would fill with the noise of my blood pumping through me like voices going on and on:

Antoinette.

Your face follows me wherever I go.

And I will restore to you the years that the locust hath eaten, the cankerworm, and the caterpillar, and the palmerworm, my great army, which I sent among you.

My sister. You are my sister, Antoinette. My dearest friend and companion.

If I could save you by my blood it would be my soul's greatest happiness.

It was January 21, 1793.

Excuse me. I mean the second day of Pluviôse, Year One, because of course they had to change everything.

Even epiphany cakes weren't to be called Cakes of the Kings anymore but Marat Cakes.

Even the cakes.

Obedient to its name, the second day of Pluviôse was cold and wet. Rain was beating on the windowpanes, drenching the citizens of Paris as they danced their ecstatic way to the guillotine with their pikes and their red hats and their drums. We sat huddled together in the Temple, unnaturally alert, as if all we had to do was listen hard enough and we could hear the sound of his feet on the steps, the sound of his breathing. He was wearing a brown overcoat and a tricorn hat with a red, white, and blue cockade. No wedding ring, having handed it over to me earlier. "I die innocent," he said. "I pardon those who have brought on my death and I pray to God—" but already the blade was falling, his lungs taking in their last gulp of air. For a moment everything was perfectly still, followed by the sound of cheering, of cannon. The Serious One fainted.

Louis the Last, they called him. And then, after, Louis the Shortened.

In his will he asked me to help our children regard the grandeur of this world, "should they be fated to encounter it," as a dangerous and transitory advantage. Help them fix their eyes instead on the lasting glory of Eternity, he implored.

The grandeur of this world. The glory of Eternity. As if the Widow Capet had any choice in the matter.

I was given black clothes to wear, whereas a Queen's mourning dress is always white. It made no difference; I never went out. I just stayed in my room and sewed, getting thinner and thinner. Like a magpie, some people said, but I thought I was more like a needle.

Outside, it was the rage for women to tie red ribbons around their necks, *à la victime,* and for men to shave their throats. Making fashion out of fear, I guess, the idea being that if you got there first, Death would have to look elsewhere.

Meanwhile yet one more escape plan was under way, involving yet more costumes, forged passports, a boat to Normandy, etc. etc. My little boy would be hidden in a basket of dirty laundry, the ever-watchful Tisons dispatched with drugged snuff. Of course it came to nothing, but since I expected nothing I wasn't disappointed.

Though maybe that isn't entirely true. Maybe it wasn't so much nothing I expected as it was the triumph of the political over the personal, of a great blundering headless behemoth over a sad little human scheme.

"The species must be looked on as a tree that is pruned without cease by an invisible hand," wrote Jacques-René Hébert, headlessness's most ardent spokesman. "Blood is the fertilizer of the plant that is called genius." He was the one who got everyone fired up with the idea of removing the bodies of France's dead Kings from their vaults in Saint-Denis and dumping them in the river.

I sent Provence Louis's wedding ring, also a lock of his hair. I sent Axel a wax impression of my seal, a homing pigeon with the words EVERYTHING GUIDES ME TO THEE. Both of them so far off and farther every day, the one near a river, the other the ocean, which might as well have been China, the moon.

Every night the same thing:

Antoinette. Antoinette.

From my heart through my pillow and into my ear.

Your face, Antoinette.

Promised a throne and then ending like this.

My little boy was sick. They took him away from me and made him a ward of the Republic. They put him in his father's old room, where I could hear him sobbing, though even that was better than later when they fed him brandy and had him sing "The Marseillaise." *To arms, citizens! Form your battalions!* Sometimes I'd catch a glimpse of him through the window, playing with other little boys, using their toy guillotines to decapitate birds and mice.

Spring came and went with its flowers and breezes. Germinal, Floréal, Prairial; Candlemas, Carnival, Lent. I couldn't eat a thing, but what I did eat went right through me, along with my blood, which every month poured out by the bucket. I would see my hand sewing at the end of my arm and it seemed to me it didn't belong to me but to one of those ancient bundles I used to make fun of, those pitiful hags with skin as gray and translucent as raw fish who used to scrabble for purchase on my sleeve, trying to catch my attention back in the days when that was what everyone wanted more than anything.

Antoinette, Antoinette.

Your Highness. Your Majesty.

Messalina, Fredegonde, Brunhild.

Madame Tison lost her mind and they took her away to the madhouse.

I hadn't lost mine, but they took me away too — not to the madhouse but to the Conciergerie, which was delicately referred to as the "waiting room." They took me away and put me in a cramped cell with a brick floor, a little fireplace, a barred window, a straw mattress, a modesty screen, and a nail in the wall where I hung my mother's watch.

Prisoner Number 280: Marie Antoinette de Lorraine d'Autriche.

Her possessions (including the aforementioned watch): A lock of her deceased husband's hair. A lock of hair from each of her four children, two dead and two still living. A sewing purse with scissors and needles and thread. A mirror. A painted miniature of the Princesse de Lamballe. Three rings. A scapular. A pair of black silk stockings. A tin box of hair pomade. A swansdown powder puff. A painted miniature of her son, Louis-Charles, ward of the Republic. His yellow glove.

They gave me a nice young girl named Rosalie to be my maid, who did her best to protect me from being watched by the two guards whenever I sat on the chamber pot, and then burned juniper berries to freshen the air afterward. She brought me linen rags to put between my legs. She brought me books. *Captain Cook's Travels. A History of Famous Shipwrecks.* She also brought her little boy, Fanfan, who was the same age as my little boy, and broke my heart.

Sometimes I'd read, sometimes I'd sew. Sometimes I'd watch the guards play backgammon, neither one of whom was very good at it. I'd drink my potion of lime-flower water, orange-flower water, maidenhair syrup, and Hofman's liquor. I'd say grace and eat my supper. Sometimes some of the other prisoners would come by to kiss my shoes.

Prisoner Number 280: bored out of her mind.

Eventually Captain Cook discovered New Caledonia, and then it was Fructidor, the days were getting shorter. In the new calendar each day was represented by a different wonder of nature, a hazelnut, a crayfish, a rose, as if Maximilien Robespierre or Jean-Paul Marat or any one of those monsters would know a crayfish if it bit him.

September 2: Crayfish. Another escape plan came to naught. To punish me I was put in an even smaller cell, a former dispensary that smelled like old medicine and piss. No window this time, no fire, no screen. No sewing purse. Water continually dripped down the walls, the same as the blood down my legs, making puddles on the floor. My shoes got mildewed but it didn't really matter since no one was coming by to kiss them anymore, having lost track of where I was. Rosalie warmed my nightgown every night over her own fire. She hung a bolt of moth-eaten carpet around my bed.

But I was cold, all the same. Cold and wet. The walls were spotted with mustard yellow lichen and dark green moss, and I couldn't help thinking of the Stairways of the Hundred Steps, which had turned out to have a hundred and five, in case anyone's interested.

I used to own two copper bathtubs, one for washing, one for rinsing. I used to sleep on six mattresses. My little boy would run in to wake me, laughing; my daughter would look up from her breviary and blink at how bright the day had grown. I used to be in love. I used to be married to a King. In my bedroom at the Petit Trianon there were three different shades of gold leaf on the ceiling.

The boxes they put me in got smaller and smaller, until the last one was so small you couldn't see it at all, or the woman inside it. Even if you were a guard. Even if you took away the screen. Where did she go? Where did she go?

Am I complaining?

No, frightened.

I was frightened.

I sat there in my chair, hour after hour, day after day, turning my rings, turning and turning them, the two guards watching my every move to make sure I wasn't up to something, meaning *playing, amusing myself,* in which case they'd have to take my rings away.

My rings. One turn to the right, and the door would swing open; another, and in would come my little boy, my little girl. Three turns, Axel. Four, Louis. Four turns to bring back the dead, their necks no longer severed, their hearts no longer stopped. Four turns and it would come to pass that the mountains drop down new wine, and the hills flow with milk, and all the rivers of Judah flow with waters, and a fountain come forth of the house of the Lord.

Whereas turn the rings to the left, and instead of a door there'd be only more wall, a daughter betrothed to the enemy, a son bearing false witness against his mother. Turn the rings to the left, and the lover would be lying in another woman's arms, the King covered with quicklime in a pauper's grave, his severed head tucked between his legs, the sun and moon dark, the stars no longer brilliant.

What's she doing? the guards asked each other. They thought it was witchcraft, I guess. Watch out, the old witch is casting a spell! Hard to believe people used to call her beautiful. Hard to believe she used to be a woman. By now they liked me well enough; they felt sorry for me. Sometimes they even brought me flowers.

Magpie. Needle. Fructidor. Vendémiaire.

Four turns to the right, and the Austrian army would take me back to Vienna.

Four turns to the left, and the box would fill with ghosts.

My hearing was still good. I could hear the nearby bells of Sainte-Chapelle perfectly, but my vision was failing, my eyes starved either for things to look at or for food. By then I was eating nothing, though I'd still say grace. Preparing to vanish, either out a door or up a chimney, which reminded me of how the old King used to climb onto the roof at Versailles and whisper down the chimney flues.

"Who are you?"

"I was called Marie Antoinette de Lorraine d'Aut-riche."

"Do you want counsel?"

"Yes."

When they finally brought me before the Revolutionary Tribunal I could scarcely see a thing. A huge dark hall, two candles, twelve jurors: a wigmaker, a cobbler, a cafe proprietor, a hatter, a printer, a musician, a lemonade seller, two carpenters, a surgeon, an ex-priest, a former marquis. Forty-one witnesses.

Who are you?

I was called Maria Antonia Josephina Johanna.

Do you want counsel?

I want my family.

My eyes failing but my ears still perfect—I could hear every whisper. *Oho, look at her now, the bitch. That'll teach her to steal our food. But why is she drumming like that on the arm of the chair?*

My mother stifling a yawn as my fingers flew across the keys of the clavichord. *Les Barricades Mystérieuses.* François Couperin. Sit straighter, Antonia. Do you want to end up with a hump?

To which the answer of course is no no no no no, unless to avoid it you have to die before the age of forty.

"Do you believe Kings are necessary for a people's happiness?"

"An individual cannot make such a decision."

The trial lasted two days. Among other things, I was accused of conspiring with my brother against France, of forcing my husband out the door and into a carriage bound for Varennes, of appointing perverse ministers, of engineering famine, of keeping the Swiss Guard in a state of perpetual drunkenness, of printing slanderous pamphlets about myself to arouse sympathy abroad, of having sex with my own son.

"Human nature cannot answer such a charge against a mother," I said. "I appeal to all the mothers in the room"—at which even the most crazed of the *tricoteuses* stood up in their red bonnets and cheered.

Naturally it didn't matter what I said.

Naturally I was found guilty.

Then it was Vendémiaire, the Feast Day of Saint Theresa, sacred to my mother, my daughter. Then it was Amaryllis, in the new calendar. A fine fresh day, a little mist, the sun trying to shine, and all the birds singing. *Two hundred thousand people have fallen in love with you,* said the Maréchal de Brissac twenty years earlier, when I made my triumphal entry into this same Parisian square. On that day, as now, people were selling cakes and lemonade. On that day, as now, everyone was in a state of high excitement.

October 16. Theresa, Amaryllis. I combed and powdered my hair. So thin, so white but with hints of fire, of who I used to be. My hair used to be beautiful. Also my eyes, also my mouth. I removed the bloody rag from between my legs, rolled it up and stuffed it in a chink in the wall. For posterity, I told myself, but I admit I was angry. Let posterity make what it would of menstrual blood. Rosalie was sobbing and to please her I ate a little bouillon. I dressed myself for the last time, in a gown of white piqué, a black slip, a muslin shawl, and my plum-colored high-heeled shoes.

When they went to bind my wrists, I put up a fight. You didn't bind my husband's wrists, I said. But when I saw the tumbril, I fell apart. My husband rode in a carriage, I told them. I squatted in the Mouse's Corner and relieved myself.

I was going. I was going.

Antonia, SIT UP STRAIGHT!

In the tumbril, riding backward, leaves and nuts raining from the trees. The sky blue now, dotted with clouds. Blue. Blue and white.

Though the soul has no spine. THE SOUL NO SPINE.

Antoinette. Antoinette.

He cut my hair, I stepped on his foot.

When you look up, clouds; when you look down, the same. Blue sky and clouds and, suddenly, water. Suddenly against the blue sky a spray of jewels.

Pardon, monsieur, I said. I did not mean to do it.

EROS

It cuts through.

Once upon a time, that's how it was. The chande-lier's facets were unpolished stone. The fountain's water was sludge in a swamp.

From the ceiling, against the sky. The shining thing cuts through. A light blooms, a current tugs, the human body works to escape its tether.

You can feel it tugging. Not love, not hope. The opposite of hope, really. There's no future in Eros, only *this*. Behind pleasure, the body moves backward.

On the palace floor a pattern of light and shadow. On the water in the basin a flicker of sun and shade.

Backward, the body says. You feel it pulling.

HALL OF MIRRORS

Through the door and up the Queen's Staircase, tap tap tap up forty-two steps. TAP TAP TAP the echo comes back, in golden rings, in rings of gold. A thin layer of dust lies everywhere. Also cobwebs, though spiders have trouble making their thread stick to marble. They have to be patient.

Patient as a spider in a mausoleum. Patient as a cat whose paws are being grilled. Over hill and dale, over moor and meadow, a million miles and a million to go. Late autumn light spills from the second-floor loggia, the smell of burning leaves, of burning houses. The planet tilts, plane trees drop their leaves; earth and clouds stream by.

It's Allhallows, it's All Souls', it's the Day Between the Years. Brumaire. BRRRRRR. It's time to fatten the pigs with acorns. It's the end of the world, where the world stops in a point like a tail.

The Room of the Queen's Guard, the Queen's Antechamber, the Salon of the Nobles, the Apartments of the Queen. Over river and stream, over valley and mountain, a million miles to the end of the world.

Meanwhile in Paris they're making things pure. Meanwhile in Paris the cats are eating the cats. Sssssss-boom. Sssssss-boom. Saint Guillotine. The Black Widow. Wasn't it Mirabeau who said that liberty is a bitch who likes to be bedded on a mattress of cadavers?

Try to be nice, though, try to be nice. It's the Reign of Purity, after all, also known as the Reign of Terror. Most people look better painted on walls. The Sun King, risen like a god to the ceiling of the Hall of Mirrors, surrounded by blue sky, clouds, the sun breaking through.

From the Salon of Peace to the Hall of Mirrors, in its seventeen windows the sun breaking through.

Seventeen windows, forty-four panes of glass each. Seven hundred forty-eight panes of glass and through them all the November sun shines on poor lonely Latona and her frog companions, the fountain dry as a bone, the basin full of leaves and in the distance the Grand Canal like a long gray finger pointing at a pair of nondescript poplars.

Tap tap tap on the parquet floor. TAP TAP TAP the echo comes back. Gold November sun, thick with dust and the illusion of heat, dripping off the crystal pendants of the chandeliers. Raindrops, teardrops. Twenty-two chandeliers hanging from the ceiling, twenty-four on pedestals along the walls. Forty-six chandeliers in all.

Spades and hearts, power and courage; clubs and diamonds, money and pleasure. Bacchus and Venus and Hermes and Modesty. If only we knew how to see green things, see them as though in bloom, in their wonder! A cord from the center of the heart, a cloud of birds from the corners of the sky.

Over earth and sea, over moon and sun. Two poplars, a million birds.

Two hundred twenty steps, a million miles. From the Salon of Peace to the Salon of War, from the root to the crown, from the rock to the spring. From Versailles to Paris, from heaven to earth.

Seventeen arcades, each with eighteen mirrors. Three hundred six mirrors and in every one of them no Antoinette.